The Name is 'Zero'

Heartlines

Books by Pam Lyons

A Boy Called Simon
He Was Bad
It Could Never Be
Latchkey Girl
Danny's Girl
Odd Girl Out
Ms Perfect

Books by Anita Eires

Tug Of Love
Summer Awakening
Spanish Exchange
Star Dreamer
Californian Summer
If Only . . .
Teacher's Pet
Working Girl

Books by Mary Hooper

Love Emma XXX
Follow That Dream
My Cousin Angie
Happy Ever After
Opposites Attract

Books by Barbara Jacobs

Two Times Two

Books by Jane Pitt

Loretta Rose
Autumn Always Comes
Stony Limits
Rainbows For Sale

Books by Ann de Gale

Island Encounter
Hands Off

Books by Anthea Cohen

Dangerous Love

Books by David S. Williams

Give Me Back My Pride
Forgive and Forget

Books by Jill Young

Change Of Heart

Books by Ann Ruffell

Friends For Keeps
Secret Passion

Books by Lorna Read

Images
The Name Is 'Zero'

Books by Jane Butterworth

Spotlight On Sam

Heartlines

Lorna Read

The Name Is 'Zero'

A Pan Original

First published 1986 by Pan Books Ltd,
Cavaye Place, London SW10 9PG
9 8 7 6 5 4 3 2 1
© Lorna Read 1986
ISBN 0 330 29182 3
Printed and bound in Great Britain by
Hunt Barnard Printing, Aylesbury, Bucks

Chapter One

It was an argument with my friend Kate about an advertisement that started it all.

'Oh, I couldn't,' I insisted, turning away from the college noticeboard. 'I'm not good enough.'

'Well, I think you are,' she encouraged.

'Nice of you to say so, but . . . well, I've never played in public. I just couldn't!' I protested.

'This wouldn't exactly be *public*,' she pointed out. 'And you don't have to be that good.'

'Huh – thanks!' I responded shortly. 'Now come on, let's forget all this nonsense. We've got a class right now, unless you've forgotten, and you know what Gina Smith's like when you're late!'

'Don't remind me,' Kate said dramatically, rolling her eyes. Clutching our bags full of books, we fled down the corridor, up the echoing concrete stairs, and were the very last to take our seats . . . but two seconds ahead of Gina, fortunately for us.

Gina was taking us for Commerce today, which was mostly the very boring history of the commercial world. While she waffled on about early banking systems, my mind wandered back to that announcement on the board.

Anyone who can play an instrument and would like to get together for the purpose of music-making is invited to a meeting in Room 27 at 5 p.m. on Thursday, was how it read and, in spite of what I'd said to Kate, I was interested and intrigued. I did play an instrument—the guitar – though I didn't reckon I was much good.

Then I had another thought; perhaps they meant classical music. I didn't have a clue about that! The music I liked was rock and pop, and a bit of American country-flavoured stuff, but not much else. And I hated jazz!

'. . . this could be termed the very beginning of the system of paying interest. *What* country are we in at the moment, Shona?'

'Uh?' My blank face betrayed the fact that, like our lecturer, I'd been miles away – but unfortunately in a different continent, for when I hazarded the guess of India, everyone burst out laughing, particularly Keith Randall, who always liked to see a girl being made a fool of.

'I can see we'll never make a bank manager out of you,' Gina said sarcastically, and everybody sniggered again, even Kate, I was horrified to see. So much for having mates, if they deserted you in your hour of misfortune and disgrace.

'You know what she's like,' Kate remarked consolingly afterwards, tucking her arm through mine as we walked in the direction of the cafeteria. 'She always has to find someone new to pick on every day. Today it was just your turn. It'll probably be mine tomorrow.'

'It's about time it was Keith Randall's,' I observed gloomily. 'Who wants to do a bloody secretarial and business course, anyway? Where's it going to get us? A job sitting in some dusty back office, keeping ledgers and getting cross-eyed over millions of figures all day? How incredibly boring!'

'Where's your imagination?' Kate retorted. 'Why are you always so gloomy and doomy?'

'Because the *world* is!' I declaimed dramatically, whirling round and bashing some bloke I didn't know with my elbow. I got him right in the midriff, and he let out a pained '*Oof!*'

'S-sorry,' I stammered embarrassedly. Kate had flushed scarlet and was biting her lip, trying not to laugh.

'Watch where you're flippin' well going,' the boy grunted. Unfortunately he was quite tasty, I noted. Pity – because now I'd made an enemy of him for ever, and had been labelled a clumsy idiot into the bargain.

We opened the door of the cafeteria and the blast of noise hit us immediately. 'Fat chance of finding a table in there!' Kate snorted. 'Come on . . .'

We were just backing out when I noticed that there *was* a table – if we didn't mind sharing it with the vile Keith Randall! 'You're right – let's go,' I agreed.

We walked off down the busy street and suddenly Kate nudged me in the ribs. 'Fancies himself, doesn't he?' she hissed. I followed the direction in which she was looking and saw the bloke I'd bashed earlier, gazing into a shop window. It was really funny, I thought; I'd never seen this boy before today, yet now I was practically falling over him everywhere I went.

'Wake up! I'm hungry, even if you aren't,' Kate reminded me. She grabbed the strap of my shoulder bag and tugged me in the direction of a side street which contained a rather grotty café that was used by a lot of students because they were quite generous with their sandwich fillings and their portions of spaghetti and pie, and didn't seem to mind requests for bizarre combinations like tuna, celery and peanut butter in a sesame seed bun. Which was lucky, because that was my current craze.

'What are you doing tonight?' Kate asked me, chomping into her cheese salad.

'I suppose I ought to be doing some shorthand practice,' I replied, knowing how unconvinced I sounded.

'Then you've got no excuse.' She beamed at me.

'No excuse for what?' I queried, wrinkling my brow at her.

'For not going along to Room 27. I'll come with you for moral support.'

'But that's on Thursday,' I reminded her.

'My digital watch tells me that it's one forty-seven on Thursday the twenty-fourth,' she intoned. I was sick of hearing what her blasted digital watch said. It was never a quarter to or a quarter past the hour any more, it was fifteen and forty-five. Quarters had ceased to exist!

'How could I have forgotten it's Thursday,' I said, 'when we've got Pete Darby this afternoon?'

Our concerted sighs ruffled the lettuce leaves on Kate's plate. Just over half an hour later, we were gazing adoringly at the lean, hungry features of our English teacher . . . and at five, I was following Kate's long mane of glossy brown hair into Room 27.

Chapter Two

There were loads of people there — far more than I would have imagined — and I recognized quite a few of them. There was Dave Simmonds, who was on a language course learning German and French — Kate fancied him. Then there was a girl called Joss who came to our shorthand, typing and word-processing classes. We'd never been particularly friendly with her because she was rather stand-offish and was always distributing leaflets about women's rights. She had a very butch, short haircut and strode around in baggy dungarees and clumpy, scuffed footgear that looked like cast-off army boots. I could never imagine anyone fancying *her*.

My eyes continued to rove furtively around the room at the mixture of eager and sceptical faces. Suddenly, I was aware that Kate had tensed up. She leant over and hissed in my ear, 'Look, it's him again. He seems to be haunting us today!'

I followed her gaze and saw, about to come through the door, the guy I'd been bumping into all day. I watched, trying to pretend I wasn't looking, as he found a space by the wall and leant against it and folded his arms. He wasn't spectacularly good-looking, but he was nice now that he wasn't scowling. His hair was short and thick and cut spikily on top. It wasn't fair and it wasn't brown, but somewhere in between. His eyes . . . no, I couldn't make them out. They might be grey though, I decided. I looked quickly away, before he sussed out that I was staring at him.

Someone shut the door with a bang and I jumped. The hubbub ceased abruptly and Mike Broadway, a final-year music student who was rumoured to be a brilliant composer, started to address us.

'First of all, I must say I'm pleased to see so many musical ladies here tonight,' he said.

'Male chauvinist pig,' muttered a voice on my right and I turned my head and saw Joss glowering. But I soon realized it wasn't just his words that had rated her disapproval but the fact that his eyes were lingering on Cathy Edgworth who, as usual, was dressed in the shortest microskirt and the skimpiest top I'd seen anywhere.

Mike expounded his aim in calling the meeting, which was to try to gather some groups of people who were musically suited to each other, get them playing together, and then stage an end-of-year concert for the whole college. He said he would come round and talk to us all individually, to find out who played what, and how well.

'Here's where I scarper. Coming?' I asked Kate, tugging at the sleeve of her sweatshirt.

'No. This could be fun,' she said.

'But you don't even play anything,' I reminded her.

'You wait and see,' she told me mysteriously.

Sure enough, as Mike headed for us and I cowered behind her, trying to turn myself into the Invisible Woman, I heard her say brightly, in answer to Mike's enquiry, 'Isn't everyone looking for the next Lennon and McCartney, and Tim Rice and Andrew Lloyd-Webber? Well, here I am!'

'Fine,' said Mike. 'I'm sure lots of people are looking for new songs. Bring some along to the next meeting. Now, how about you?'

'Oh, Shona plays the guitar and sings and she's really good,' Kate babbled, dropping me right in it.

'Great! Bring it along on Monday, then, and we'll see what you can do,' he said cheerfully, and I could have flattened her.

I said as much to her as we walked from the bus stop towards the house in Wavertree where she and her parents lived. My bedsitter was only a couple of roads away and I spent a lot of time with Kate and her parents, who were always inviting me round for meals. My own parents lived on the other side of the river, in Heswall, too far away for me to travel every day, which was why they'd reluctantly given their permission for me to get a bedsit – though they'd made sure it was all above board by coming over and vetting the landlady and making sure there were no single males under the age of sixty in any of the other rooms!

'I'm not going on Monday and that's that,' I grumbled as Kate opened her front door. 'If you think I'm getting up and making a fool of myself in front of all those people –'

'Look,' she retorted hotly, 'why won't you believe anyone who says you're good? You are! You need me to push you, even if it means *I've* got to make an idiot of myself by bashing out some dreadful lyrics.' She stopped and smiled. 'I'm gonna make you a star, kid,' she said in a phoney American accent and I thumped her as we stumbled into the front room to interrupt her parents' TV programme.

I went home to spend the weekend with my own family and completely forgot my forthcoming ordeal until Kate called round for me on Monday morning.

'Right. Where is it, then?' she said briskly.

'Where's what?' I asked dumbly.

'Your guitar – or had you forgotten, accidentally-on-purpose?'

She pushed past me into my room, grabbed the encased instrument from its hidey-hole at the side of the book-case and marched out with it. We didn't speak to each other again till lunchtime, I was so mad. And as I stood in Room 27 that evening, waiting for Mike Broadway, my hands were icy and clammy and my stomach felt as though a giant boa constrictor was writhing round inside it. I didn't *want* to play my guitar in front of anyone – why couldn't Kate understand? I thought in panic. But then it was too late. Mike was in, the door was shut and all around people were unfastening zips and buckles and revealing all manner of strange and wonderful musical instruments.

Soon, the air was full of the twanging sounds of electric guitars being tuned, and as the first few chords and runs were plucked, I was relieved to find out that I wasn't the only person who played duff notes occasionally. Heartened, I unwrapped my own guitar, then, hearing a sudden ripple of piano notes, I searched the room, puzzled because I knew there was no piano there. To my surprise, I found that the source of the delightful, complex melody was Joss, standing over some kind of electronic keyboard which she'd laid on a table top.

Interested, Kate and I went over to her and she

grinned at us and went on playing. Infectious rhythms were being beaten out on a set of bongo drums nearby. The owner of the flying hands was Ireka Jameson, a bubbly West Indian girl with the craziest laugh and hair braided in thick sausages laced with ribbon. Kate and I knew her slightly as, like us, she was keen on swimming, and so we often saw her and her friends at the baths.

By some miracle, my guitar was in tune with Joss's keyboard and I began to strum soft chords while she played. A tall girl in old jeans and a baggy shirt brought a bass guitar over and began to pluck out notes, and the sounds we were making began to mingle with the cacophony gradually filling the room.

But we could just about make out what we were playing, so we continued. Our tune was recognizable now – Michael Jackson's old song, *Ain't No Sunshine*. I knew it well, so I began to sing. Suddenly, from behind me, some really nice lead guitar lines appeared and when I saw who was responsible, I was completely taken aback and stopped singing. It was the mystery boy, the victim of the flying elbow. And he really could play!

'Go on . . .' he encouraged me and I was just opening my mouth when Mike yelled and banged on the table and called the din to a halt. He suggested that it might be better if we didn't all play at once unless we were all playing the same tune. He added that the college authorities had agreed that we could use three rooms, so it was up to us to split practice times between us.

'I think you've got a great voice. What's your name?'

I snatched my attention away from Mike and onto

the demon guitarist. 'Shona,' I supplied. 'And yours?'

'Rob. Rob Kemp. Hey, have you ever tried playing an electric guitar?'

I shook my head, not wanting to speak while Mike was still talking. Then Mike finished his speech.

'Here – have a go.' Rob placed his guitar in my hands and I almost dropped it, it was so heavy.

'I'd be like the Hunchback of Notre Dame in no time if I played one of these,' I joked.

'Go on . . . try,' he encouraged. 'It's easy. With a strong voice like yours, you ought to learn.'

I tentatively touched a string. The noise it made was much louder than I'd expected and made me jump. Rob reached out and turned the volume control down. I formed a D Major chord and strummed it softly and thought how nice it sounded. Maybe he had a point.

I handed it back to him. 'Maybe one day I'll be able to afford one,' I said.

'I'll let you have another go next Thursday,' he said, grinning. His eyes weren't grey, I observed, but a sort of hazelly-brown. They were warm eyes, sparkly eyes, eyes that made me want to keep on gazing into them. But I was forced to pull myself away by Kate, who wanted to set off in pursuit of Dave Simmonds.

'See you Thursday then,' Rob said. Then he ruined absolutely everything by adding, 'And I'd leave that old thing at home, if I were you.'

'How dare you!' squeaked Kate, pretending he had meant her. But there was a hot, angry flush on my face as I clutched my guitar close. How *dare* he insult my precious instrument! I'd learned to play on it, I was as fond of it as I was of . . . of Kate! I never wanted to

14

speak to him again, nice eyes or no nice eyes, and if I met him in the corridor, I was going to make sure he received another 'accidental' bashing!

Chapter Three

It was while Kate and I were indulging in a fantasy about a passionate affair between Pete Darby and Cathy Edgworth that I found out more about what Joss was like – to my cost. We'd noticed a red mark on Pete's neck that we were sure was a love-bite.

'Cathy's probably a five-hundred-year-old vampire really,' I sniggered. 'They have midnight trysts in the cathedral graveyard and she sucks his blood.'

Kate disguised a giggle as a choking cough, because Darby was looking pointedly in our direction, but just then the bell went to indicate the end of the lesson. That's when Joss struck.

'Honestly, what a pair of infants you two are,' she announced haughtily. She'd been sitting behind us, wearing her usual army surplus gear, with something that looked like an old green sock tied round her bristly brown hair. 'Anyone would think you were about twelve. *Some* people come to these classes to *learn*.' With that, she swept off leaving us staring after her.

'That girl has *no* sense of humour,' I declared.

'You're right,' Kate agreed. 'She may be a good

musician, but that's absolutely all she has to recommend her. What a weirdo!'

We decided to avoid the canteen and were dashing down the pavement, threading our way between shoppers and office workers as we headed for our favourite café, when something happened which made me, at least, forget all about stuffy Joss. Someone male began yelling my name and Kate clutched my arm, dragging me to a halt. 'Shona! It's that Rob!' she shrieked in disbelief.

We waited for him to catch up with us and I reminded myself how angry I was with him.

'I waited for you outside Room 17, Shona,' he said accusingly. 'I thought that was where the English classes always were.'

'They would be normally, but the radiators are on the blink so they had to find us somewhere else,' I explained frostily.

He ran a hand through his fairish hair which looked blonder in natural light. 'I bumped into Jonathan Stokes and he said he'd seen you leave the building, so I dashed after you. The thing is –' he was totally leaving Kate out of the conversation, I noticed '– I wondered if you'd like a proper lesson on my electric guitar? I've been playing for some time and I've got one of those Teach Yourself cassettes, if that's any help.'

I stared at him. If he possessed an ounce of sensitivity he must know he'd insulted me the other night. Was this an attempt to make it up to me?

'Well . . .' I began, 'it's very nice of you to offer.'

Without thinking, we were letting our footsteps take us slowly but unerringly in the direction of *Mario's*, our lunchtime rendezvous.

'Hi! Fancy bumping into you!' a cheery voice hailed us and Kate cursed out loud, as well she might, because the person approaching the door of the café from the opposite direction was fat, horrible, leering Keith Randall, his hair, as usual, looking as if it needed a good wash.

'Hi, mate,' Rob responded, the only one of us to bother to make a reply.

'Just in time to make up a foursome, I see. Which one are you with?' Keith burbled. I found myself imagining the earful Joss would have given him.

As usual, the café was crowded with students and I felt really sorry for poor Kate who had to sit with Keith all squashed up next to her. It must have really put her off her egg and chips as Keith told weak, revolting jokes like, 'Did you hear about the legless cowboy who was only a low-down bum?' I was able to tune out most of it as Rob was talking about the rock musicians he admired.

'Of the old school, I think Jeff Beck's about the best. He's got such feel. He hasn't got the fireworks Jimi Hendrix had, but he makes up for it in other ways.' I nodded sagely. I hadn't heard of either of them.

'So this nun went back across the same field, see –'

I gave Kate a glance of sympathy as Keith droned on.

'So how about the guitar lessons? I'm quite serious, you know. I think you'd pick it up really quickly.'

I snatched my attention back to Rob again. I didn't really know what to say. Half of me wanted to retort that I was quite happy playing my old acoustic guitar, and the rest of me . . . well, that brief try-out I'd had on

Rob's electric guitar had been very exciting.

He reached for the sugar, to spoon some into his cup of tea, and as he did so, his hand accidentally brushed mine and I felt my skin tingle as if with a sudden attack of pins and needles. I was trying to figure out why when Kate suddenly clapped a hand over her mouth.

'Oh, no – I've forgotten to get that book I need for my essay tonight. I'd better dash to the shop. Coming, Shona?'

I rapidly considered. If I stayed, Keith would collar me and I'd have to listen to all his stupid jokes. If I went, Rob might think I'd turned down his offer. But, on the other hand, if I stayed he might think I was interested in him for other reasons, too, and I most certainly wasn't. Boys definitely didn't figure on my agenda at the moment. I had a sort of boyfriend at home, a bloke called Darryl whom I'd known all my life. Things had never got really romantic between us, but I had my hopes. So, getting up, I said goodbye to the boys and followed Shona out. But something made me risk a quick look back as I reached the door and I was vaguely miffed to find Rob was already deep in conversation with Keith, as if he didn't care about my leaving at all . . .

They say strange happenings never come singly. I had my second that afternoon during touch-typing practice. As I walked in, Joss looked up as if she'd been waiting for me.

'Shona . . . Just the person,' she announced briskly. 'I'm having a few people round to my place tonight and I'd like you to come and bring your guitar. We'll have a sing-song and a Chinese take-away, okay?'

She started scribbling something on a pad — her address, I assumed — as if there was no earthly chance I would turn down her invitation. Fine hostess she was, if she couldn't even be bothered to provide food, I thought scornfully. She handed me the scrap of paper torn from her shorthand notebook, shot me a quick grin which disappeared almost as soon as it formed, and sat down again with a 'See you later, then.'

'What was all that about?' Kate asked after class. She'd come in late and seen Joss hand me her address. 'Trying to get you to join her Women Against Unfair Treatment of Garden Slugs action group, or something?'

'Almost,' I chuckled. 'She's invited me to dinner, though the Chinko round the corner's cooking it!'

'Rather you than me,' Kate replied with a shudder. 'It'll be a mega-bore occasion, if you ask me. I hope you said you couldn't make it?'

I grimaced. 'My brain didn't work in time. I can't get out of it now.'

'Yes you can. Say you've got a prior arrangement to have tea with my parents and I've only just reminded you.'

'Hey, that's a good one!' I said admiringly, and looked round for Joss, but she'd vanished. I looked in the cafeteria, the library, even the loo, but she was nowhere to be found — and I was stuck with having to turn up at 61 Ransome Street at eight o'clock, or else!

Chapter Four

Ransome Street was a real slum. One end of it had been knocked down. Maybe it had happened during the war and they just hadn't got round to rebuilding on the site. Half the remaining houses were boarded up, and those that weren't looked like squats. Joss's house stood out from the others only because it had a large CND poster in the downstairs window.

The bells weren't labelled and as I stood there wondering which one to press, I noticed that the door was slightly ajar, so I pushed it open and stepped inside an uncarpeted, mouldy-smelling hallway. I grazed my hip against the handlebar of a rusty old bike as I made for the staircase.

'Hey . . . Joss?' I called up the stairs. 'Anybody there?'

There was no response, so I shouted a bit louder and at last I heard her voice echoing down.

'It's right at the top, I'm afraid. Come on up!'

My knees felt quite trembly by the time I reached the top of the fourth flight of stairs, and I made a mental note to take more exercise and get myself fitter. A newly painted, bright blue door stood open and a buzz of conversation and music came out to greet me.

The room I entered was both interesting and cosy, with brightly coloured rugs scattered over the floor and absolutely loads of books and pictures all over the place. I spotted Ireka sitting crosslegged on the floor, one gleaming brown arm resting on a small set of drums; the tall, gangling girl who had played the bass guitar the other night was standing over by the window. A woman in a long Indian dress with embroidery on the bodice sat on a wooden chair holding a small baby on her lap while Joss herself was pouring wine into glasses, aided by a mate of hers called Jancis who was doing a degree course in something called Humanities.

'You know Jancis, don't you?' Joss said and I nodded. 'That's Pip who was playing with us the other night –' She indicated the tall girl who shook back her lank blonde locks and smiled, '– and this is my downstairs neighbour Maggie, and baby Simon.'

Various grunting, squeaking noises were coming from the bundle on Maggie's lap. I love babies and I couldn't resist walking over and peeping at the red face sticking out of the yellow towelling Babygro.

'How old is he?' I enquired.

'Three months,' she replied. 'Think you can lullaby him to sleep? He's being a little devil tonight.'

I told her I hoped so and accepted the glass of red wine which Joss offered me.

'Take a seat,' she invited, though it was more of an order really, and I parked myself in a chair behind Ireka, right beneath a poster advertising some feminist talk entitled *Man Is The Enemy*. I was surprised she even allowed little Simon in the room!

Joss's electric keyboard was lying on the floor next to my chair and a lead trailed from it to a small amplifier. I reached down and touched a key but nothing happened; it obviously wasn't switched on.

'Well, now that we're all here, how about some

music?' Joss said cheerfully. 'I thought we all sounded quite good together the other night, but it was hard to tell with all that row going on, so I thought I'd organize this little private get-together.'

It was Rob who had contributed most to what we had been playing that evening, I reflected. Why hadn't he been invited tonight? But I thought I already knew the answer — it was printed in three-inch-high letters above my head.

Rather reluctantly, I unzipped my guitar case, got my instrument out and asked Joss to play some notes on her keyboard so that I could check that I was in tune with her. Ireka, elbows sticking out at crazy angles, began tapping out amazing rhythms on her drums. Pip tuned up her bass, while Joss played light, feathery runs and scales. Maggie's baby was quiet now, his eyes wide in fascination.

We found a song we all knew and launched into it. We must have gone on for well over half an hour, until suddenly we all seemed to come to a halt more or less together, Pip's bass guitar petering out, my aching fingers practically dropping off the guitar strings.

'Wow-*ee*!' Joss exploded. 'That was great. Well, what do you think, Shona? Do you think we'll make a group?'

Her unexpected question made me sit up so sharply that I banged my elbow on the table. 'Ouch, that hurt! A group . . .? I – I hadn't really thought about it,' I faltered. Did I want to be in a group? Did I have the time? Was it just fun, or did they seriously want to get somewhere? These were the kind of questions whizzing round inside my head.

'Oh, let's give it a try,' Ireka said eagerly, her eyes shining.

'I thought you sounded really good together,' Maggie put in, and Jancis agreed.

'We can practise round here. Maggie lives downstairs and she wouldn't mind, would you, Mags?'

'No, as long as I can come up and listen properly,' she replied, smiling.

'Jancis is a bit of an artist on the quiet – she can do our posters,' Joss added.

I looked at them all. What did I have in common with them, apart from music? But maybe that was enough. 'Well . . . all right, I'll give it a try,' I said, and instantly we were all on our feet and jumping around the room. Then we went off to get our take-away – just as well, because I was starving!

'Hey, Kate, guess what?' I greeted my mate the next day. 'I'm in a group! Joss and Pip and Ireka and me –'

'Which one's Pip? Olive Ostrich, do you mean?' she muttered, searching frantically for her shorthand book.

'Uh?'

'That tall, gawky one with the straggly hair?'

'Yes, that's her. You are unkind,' I complained. Gina came in just then so I had to tell Kate the rest of the details in the cafeteria later. But I was just in the middle of it all when Kate's eyes widened in disbelief. Before I had a chance to turn round and see who she was looking at, Rob was standing next to me.

'Hi, I was hoping I'd find you here,' he said, giving Kate the merest nod and concentrating on me. 'Doing anything tonight?'

I shook my head, my heart pounding at my ribcage – though I didn't know what I was getting so excited about. After all, it wasn't as if I fancied him . . .

'I thought you might like that electric guitar lesson that I promised you,' he offered. 'What time do you finish today?'

'Er . . . four o'clock,' I replied, wondering why my voice was sounding all weak and wavery.

'I'll see you in here, then. You can come back to my place and we'll have something to eat and make a musical evening of it.'

He seemed to be taking it for granted that I'd come. Kate was smirking all over her face.

'Right,' I managed to reply.

'Must go, I'm late,' he said, 'see you later,' and strode off towards the door without a backward glance.

'Uh-oh, love in the air,' Kate said smugly.

'Rubbish!' I retorted.

'No, idiot, I don't mean you. Over there!' she ordered, nodding to our right. I looked – and there was Gina Smith sitting at a table with Pete Darby, deep in conversation.

'You don't think they might go off for a romantic walk in the park and cancel our class?' I mused hopefully. But no such luck. Darby got to his feet and we had to speed along the corridor to get to the classroom before him.

As I was packing my books and notes away afterwards, Joss came up and asked if I could manage to make a rehearsal that night.

'Sorry, I can't,' I told her.

'Oh.' She looked quite taken aback – and very disapproving. 'Tomorrow . . .?'

'Tomorrow's Mike's music night and I really think we ought to go,' I reminded her.

'Friday I've got a women's group meeting . . . it'll have to be Saturday,' she said. 'At least it might give us time to think up some song ideas.'

'I hope so,' I agreed. I didn't know why I found myself reluctant to tell her I was seeing Rob. After all, she would have approved of my having a guitar lesson, surely? But I knew how her mind worked and I didn't want it working that way. There were some things I wanted to keep private and unspoiled . . .

Chapter Five

'This knob's for sustain,' Rob explained. 'And this is bass tone, and this one's treble. But you can alter lots of things over at the amplifier, too. And then there's effects units. I've got a fuzz and a flanger –'

'A what?' I asked, absolutely fascinated. Rob started to explain what the various musical accessories did, and I felt completely blinded by science. I couldn't make head or tail of the technical information he was giving me, but when I said as much to Rob, he told me it didn't matter how they worked, as all I needed to know was the kind of sound each one made.

I was desperate for a demonstration, but he insisted on putting the guitar in my hands and making me have a go. It was completely different to playing an acoustic guitar. The first thing I noticed was that the strings were much more bendy, and you had to be a lot more accurate because every sound you made came out so loud. It was a whole different style of playing really, but soon I was really getting into it.

I started singing, rather diffidently at first, but Rob encouraged me to go on, and then began singing a harmony which sounded really great.

'I think you ought to be in the band, too. I'm going to ask the others,' I said excitedly. I'd told him about Joss's plans.

'Well . . . it would be nice,' Rob said wistfully.

'Musical evening' was an understatement for that session which started before five and went on till almost eleven, at which point he said we'd better pack up or his landlord would chuck him out. We didn't even stop to eat!

'Will you get home all right?' he asked, with an anxious note in his voice.

'Well . . .' I hesitated. It *was* quite late . . .

'Tell you what, I'll walk you to the bus stop,' he offered, plucking his leather jacket off the back of a chair.

We didn't stop talking about music all the way to the bus stop. Unfortunately, the bus came almost at once – they never do that when you're desperately waiting for one, of course – and just as I was about to step onto it, Rob leaned forward and brushed his warm, dry lips against my cheek. The surprise caused me to take my hand off the rail, whereupon the conductor, in a broad Scouse accent, yelled, 'Make yer mind up, luv – are youse getting on or not?'

'Go on.' Rob gave me a little push and, dazed, I stumbled down the aisle and found a seat. By the time I glanced back through the window, Rob was just a speck in the distance, lit by the orange glow of a street lamp.

I scrabbled about in my bag and found my small make-up mirror and gazed at my reflection. My face was so flushed, it was almost crimson – I have very blonde hair just like my father's and my skin is so fair that I have to watch it in the sun or else I go scarlet. And another disadvantage my skin type has is that it shows every flush of emotion.

I felt ashamed and hoped Rob hadn't noticed my rosy glow. He *would* get the wrong idea!

My hair, which refused to wave or curl no matter what I did to it, looked all tousled and windswept. Even the collar of my jacket was crumpled. How could Rob have kissed someone who looked such a sight? But it wasn't a proper kiss, I reminded myself sternly. Then it occurred to me that he hadn't had to do it. Something must have inspired him. Or had he been brought up to give people social pecks? Perhaps I reminded him of his sister, or a cousin. In that case, I was quite safe.

But safe from what? What was I scared of? If Rob made any advances, all I'd have to do was turn him down. I'd done it before, to other boys. I certainly would turn Rob down, too, after the sneering way he'd treated my guitar and my playing. Yet he *had* been trying to help me, I realized, and he must have a reason; but, if all he wanted was to get off with me, there were much easier and more straightforward ways of going about it.

The bus's brakes screeched and we lurched to a halt and I recognized the traffic lights by Penny Lane. Good job I'd noticed, because I had to get off here to change buses. Trying to puzzle Rob out had nearly caused me a very long walk.

I couldn't sleep properly that night. My pulse was racing and my mind was working overtime. Eventually, I dozed off and when I woke up bleary-eyed next morning I debated whether or not to take the day off and stay in bed. But I knew Kate would be worried about me – and besides, it was Thursday, which meant music night, and anything could happen!

So I struggled unwillingly in to college and at lunchtime I filled Kate in on the events of the previous night – all of them.

'I think if a guy gives you *any* kind of kiss it means he's interested in you,' Kate said, with a mischievous smirk. 'I'd watch it if I were you, Shona. I bet he'll ask you out!'

I tossed my head. 'Well, the answer won't be yes,' I prophesied.

He certainly didn't ask me out that night – not that I felt disappointed. Far too many other things happened and took my mind right off my prospective love-life.

Some of the other musicians in Mike's little crew had been practising on their own, too, and there were several impromptu mini-concerts, including Joss, Pip,

Ireka and me – and Rob, who joined in without being asked, which earned him some fearful scowls from Joss. I felt really sorry for him. I hadn't mentioned Joss's get-together and the fact that men were a touchy subject with her.

When we'd finished, we got a round of applause from the others, even though we'd only played an old Beatles song.

Mike came over to us. 'Four girls and one guy – that's quite an original line-up,' he said. 'What are you going to call yourselves?'

'We're not –' began Joss hotly, but I cut in quickly.

'Haven't a clue,' I said brightly.

'That's going to look a bit odd on posters,' Mike chuckled. '*Thursday night, Strawberry Switchblade; Friday night, Haven't A Clue!*' Even Joss grinned at his joke.

Most of the musicians decided to go to the pub afterwards, including our lot. All except Rob, that is; when I looked for him to ask him if he was coming with us, he'd already packed up his guitar and gone.

'Maybe he felt the bad vibes Joss was giving him,' I suggested to Kate.

Indeed, the very first subject Joss brought up was him – and me!

'Pip and I have been discussing your guitar playing, Shona,' she said as we all settled ourselves round a table.

'Oh, really?' I responded warily, nudging Kate.

'Listening to Rob's playing makes me realize that we must have an electric guitar in the group. An acoustic just isn't powerful enough, it's not right.'

'Oh,' I grunted crossly. First Rob, and now Joss and Pip. I'd never *asked* for anyone to criticize my playing. I'd been quite happy playing to myself until Kate had dragged me along to these wretched music nights. It was all her fault.

'So what do you want me to do about it?' I challenged, in a tone which should have told them that I was in no mood to be ordered about.

'Learn,' Pip said earnestly, taking over from Joss. 'Honestly, your voice is great. You must get yourself an electric guitar and practise . . .'

'Have you any idea how much those things cost?' I pointed out angrily.

The others exchanged glances.

'We really do want you in the band,' Joss insisted. 'The thing is, we want it to be an all-girl band. I know Rob's very good, but he can't keep on playing with us permanently. He can join in for a time but as soon as you're good enough, Shona, you can take over.'

'She makes it all sound so cut-and-dried and easy,' I hissed in Kate's ear.

'And there's another important thing we've all got to talk about,' Joss continued. 'If we're going to be serious about our musical future, we've got to make a pact. College work first, music second, and boyfriends third. We can't have anyone saying they can't come to a rehearsal because they're going somewhere with their boyfriend and –'

'Oh, come on, Joss,' Ireka butted in, her huge dark eyes flashing sparks. 'You can't expect us to live like nuns! Lloyd and I have been going out for ages and it won't go down very well with him if I say I can only see him once a fortnight . . .'

'It's your decision,' Joss said coolly. 'Either you're ambitious and you want to be in a group and get somewhere, or else you want to tag around at some bloke's beck and call. It's up to you.'

Ireka let out an exasperated exclamation. 'In that case, I think I'll resign now.'

'Oh no – please don't, Ireka,' I begged. 'If you're giving up, so am I.'

'God, some people really are wet!' barked Joss. 'We've got the makings of something really good here. Can't you feel how well we all play together? I'm sure we could get somewhere. And it would be much better than being on the dole when we leave here!' Her voice had changed from anger to pleading, as she gazed from Ireka to me. 'Why can't we just give it a try . . .? Just a couple of weeks, to see what happens? We need to write some songs, try to get some original material together. I was hoping you'd have a go, Kate . . .'

Ireka took a swig of her white wine. 'Oh, all right then. Just for a couple of weeks. But I'm telling you now that next Tuesday's out as far as rehearsals are concerned. I definitely have got a prior engagement – and it's with Lloyd, if you must know.'

So the evening ended with all of us having agreed to meet on Saturday afternoon in Joss's flat. Kate had other things on her mind, though; Dave had asked her to go and see a film with him on Friday night.

'No snogging on the back row,' I joked. 'Don't do anything I wouldn't!'

When I met up with her on Saturday morning, she was in a terrific mood and said she'd had a fantastic evening and they were going out again. I felt a pang of jealousy. It was ages since anyone had asked me out. I hadn't even seen Darryl since I'd last been home for the weekend. But then, he was more of a friend than a boyfriend . . .

So I went along to Joss's flat on Saturday afternoon. She had asked us all to bring along any songs we'd written. I didn't have anything to offer. Although I'd racked my brains all Friday evening nothing had come to me, not even the flicker of an idea. Kate had decided not to put in an appearance as she didn't have anything ready either, also there was a chance Dave might be calling round for her.

So I dragged my much maligned guitar along and, as it turned out, had a really hilarious afternoon. Pip was bullied into starting first.

'My car wouldn't start this morning,' she wailed, trying to sound like a blues singer, 'and there's a pain in my heart this morning —'

'Try Milk of Magnesia,' suggested Ireka and we all fell about laughing.

Then Rob arrived and I suddenly felt all nervous and self-conscious, inadvertently bashed my poor guitar on the arm of the chair I was sitting on, and felt a total idiot. Fancy behaving like this just because there's a good-looking boy in the room, I scolded myself furiously. I was probably blushing again, too!

'I've seen an ad for a drum kit in the *Liverpool Echo*,' Ireka informed us all excitedly. 'I'm going round to see it tonight. It would be much better than these little drums I've been using. I can play too – my dad used to have a kit when I was a kid. I'm taking Lloyd with me so I won't get ripped off or anything.'

I guessed that remark wouldn't appeal to Joss, but so what? She couldn't expect everyone to think the same way as her . . .

Joss played us a couple of melodies she'd worked out on her keyboard, then, very shamefacedly, sang the only lyrics she'd been able to think of, which were almost as dreadful as Pip's. As songwriters, we were a hopeless bunch. It was all down to Kate, it seemed.

We played through a good few songs that afternoon. It was amazing how much better I sang when I didn't have to play as well. Rob had taken over all the guitar work and I began to wish he were a permanent fixture. Perhaps Joss would see sense.

'We still haven't thought of a name for ourselves,' Ireka reminded us eventually, pushing her braided hair off her perspiring forehead.

'Well, let's see . . . What are we? A motley collection of students of one sort or another. Five of us. Pity there's already a group called Pentangle.'

'Doesn't Pentacle mean five-pointed?' I offered.

'Sounds too much like Pentangle, or else *tentacle*. Ugh!' Ireka shuddered.

'Well, we're starting from nothing, but we can't call ourselves Nothing, it's too much of a downer,' Pip said musingly.

'Reckon Pete Darby would give us a zero for imagination if he could hear us,' I put in.

'Zero . . . Hey, that's not bad!' Joss cried. 'It's got something. Zero . . . Zero . . .' She tried it over and I must say it did have a certain ring to it. The others thought so, too.

'Shona, you're a genius,' Rob said, clapping me on the back and making me glow even more to think I'd won his praise.

'It wasn't really my idea,' I said modestly.

'Yes it was,' chorused the others.

And so Zero was born. But by the time I lugged my old guitar up the stairs of the bus that evening, I reflected that zero was about the sum total of personal interest Rob was showing in me . . .

Chapter Six

I didn't see much of Kate over the next couple of weeks – outside college, that is. She was seeing Dave and I was involved with Zero and we only managed to snatch the odd lunchtime chat and bus-ride home together. So I was delighted when she called round at my place one morning, just as I was cramming a piece of bread and marmalade into my mouth.

'What a state!' she commented as I wiped the crumbs off my face. Then she handed me a notebook. 'Er . . . I've had a go at some lyrics. Pehaps you could have a look at them and, if you think they're all right, maybe you could pass them on to Joss for me.'

'Why don't you give them to her yourself?' I enquired.

'She's been very funny with me lately. Haven't you noticed? She seems to be avoiding me.'

I had noticed, as it happened. But Joss was such a strange person that I had put it down to one of her funny moods.

I had an earlier class than Kate that day and, alone on the bus, I read through her lyrics, but with a sinking heart. No way would Joss like them – they were all love songs!

And I was right. At our rehearsal that night I handed her the book; she flipped through the pages and handed it back with a shake of her head.

'I think we can forget Kate as our lyric writer,' she said rudely. I was tempted to make a tart reply but managed to control myself, though I wished I knew what had gone wrong between her and Kate.

However, seconds later I forgot all about it because, in her usual calm fashion, Joss informed us that we'd got our first booking – playing for a social organized by one of her and Pip's women's groups!

'Wow! That's fantastic!' Ireka shrieked. 'Are we going to have to dress Rob up in drag?'

The rest of the evening was spent discussing what we should play and when I got home that night, with thoughts of Joss and Pip and women's lib in my head, I got a really great idea for a song – my first ever! It was all about the attitude of feminists towards men, and I called it *Love Thine Enemy*, after that poster of Joss's. I thought it was quite witty and satirical and when I plucked up courage to sing it to the others (scared stiff of Rob's reaction, of course!), they all seemed to approve, and even he grinned wryly.

Knowing we had a public performance coming up meant that we were rehearsing practically every night of the week. Being in this strange limbo-land with Rob, with him seeming so friendly, yet so impersonal and distant at the same time, was real torture. If only I knew what he felt about me! After every rehearsal I'd go home and lie in bed thinking over every detail of how he looked and what he said. I kept telling myself not to be so stupid and to realize that it was probable that he just didn't fancy me. Then I'd go and remember a certain way he'd looked at me, or the feel of his fingers on mine, showing me a new guitar chord, and I'd go trembly all over and feel positive that there *was* something between us. Maybe he was shy, but I knew I couldn't wait for ever or I'd go mad!

The night of our concert came round at last and I felt sick with fright as I stood backstage in the small church hall. Lots of our friends had promised to pay the entrance fee and swell the numbers. I was very relieved to discover that men were welcome, otherwise we *might* have had to stick some lipstick on Rob and hide a couple of oranges under his tee-shirt!

I found that once I actually started singing, my nerves miraculously melted away. We didn't play many wrong notes — well, not *that* many! — and the audience actually seemed to be enjoying it. Maybe my ears were deceiving me, perhaps it was only wishful thinking, but I was sure they clapped hardest of all after my *Love Thine Enemy* song. I came off stage on a real high and we all hugged each other and there was a really good, united feeling between us for the first time.

And getting a hug from Rob made me feel even happier.

As we were packing our instruments away in the van which Pip had borrowed from her cousin, a gang of our friends including Kate and Dave, and Keith Randall and his friend Li, a small Chinese boy who looked even more minute next to Keith, came rushing over to us. Keith spoke first. 'I honestly thought you were going to be lousy,' he said bluntly. 'I closed my eyes and gritted my teeth when you came on stage, expecting to be thoroughly embarrassed –'

'Gee, thanks . . .' drawled Joss acidly.

'Oh ye of little faith!' Rob muttered. Then he winked at me and I felt as if I'd been struck by a charge of electricity; I had to look away from him or else I knew I'd blush.

' – but once you'd started playing, I had to take it all back,' Keith was saying. 'You were really good. Congrats!' He shook our hands energetically and Li nodded to us all, grinning, and then the strange duo made their way back to their seats, Keith's padded bomber jacket making him look even huger than he was.

Dave clapped Rob on the back. 'Great sound,' he said. 'And I never realized you had such a good voice,' he added, turning to me. Now I really *was* blushing!

After the show we all went to the pub, just in time for one drink before closing.

'Shona . . . I'm sorry we haven't seen much of each other lately,' Kate apologized. 'What with me and Dave, and you and Zero . . .'

'I know,' I replied, glugging my cool lager.

'If you're free on Saturday night, maybe we could get together – me and Dave, and you and . . . Well, how are things going with Rob?'

'Badly. In fact, not at all,' I informed her, realizing it was days since we'd had the chance of a good heart-to-heart. Rob was talking to Keith, Dave and Li at the bar, so I was quite safe.

Kate put her hand on my arm and touched me consolingly. 'I'm sorry. I could've sworn, from the way I saw him looking at you on stage –'

'Oh, that's just part of the act,' I said hollowly. 'We *have* to look as if we all like each other, don't we?'

Dave approached just then and asked if I'd like a lift back with them. I accepted gladly, and Kate was tactful enough not to mention Rob again on the way home. But her words had set me thinking. Had Rob really been giving me special looks? Was he sending me signals that I was being too dense to pick up? Why, oh why, didn't he *say* something . . .?

Chapter Seven

By the following Wednesday, I knew Kate must have got it all wrong, because Rob and I were right in the middle of a steaming row and I'd never felt so miserable. Yet I had been the one who, quite unwittingly, had started it . . .

'We've just got to get some decent original songs into our act,' I'd stated categorically. 'We're never going to get anywhere if we don't.'

'Your song is witty enough, but you could have made it better if you'd spent a bit longer on it, Shona,' Rob scolded.

I felt myself freeze inside. Why hadn't he said something when he'd first heard it, why wait until now, when it was actually part of our repertoire and I couldn't change it without messing up everybody who'd learned the words?

'Your friend Kate's a good writer. Has she done anything else?' Rob enquired.

I immediately looked at Joss, and caught the frown she exchanged with Pip. Then I decided I wasn't going to let Rob just condemn my skills out of hand. I *wanted* to be a good songwriter. How dare he discourage me like this?

'I've got plenty of ideas kicking around in my notebook –' I began.

'Ideas are no good,' Rob said cuttingly. 'I can't set an *idea* to music. What I need is a complete set of lyrics, because I'm better at tunes than I am at words.'

'Same here,' Joss put in.

'I'm never going to write another song,' I hurled. 'I've been trying and trying to produce something original for Zero, and if you're too pig-headed even to discuss my ideas . . .'

Tears were welling up in my eyes as I slammed out of the room and into the kitchen. I was just sipping a glass of water and trying to calm myself down when the door opened and I thought, with an instant surge of wild hope, that it might be Rob and that this could be the confrontation I'd been dreaming of. He'd come in to apologize, find me in tears, throw his arms around me to comfort me, and then . . .

But it was Ireka, not Rob, who came in to see if I was okay. 'Don't take any notice of him,' she pleaded. 'I think he's feeling hen-pecked or something today. And *I* like your songs,' she added soothingly.

'Thanks.' I smiled wanly. 'You've only ever heard one, though – and that's all anyone's ever going to hear. With a few ill-chosen put-downs, Rob Kemp has ruined my creativity for good. I don't want to discuss writing songs ever again!'

'Hmph! Artistic temperament,' grunted a sarcastic voice from the door, and I looked up at Joss, who scowled. 'Maybe having a man in the group wasn't such a good idea, after all.'

A bolt of alarm shot through me. Surely she wasn't suggesting kicking him out? She turned and went back into the living-room and I didn't dare say any more about it. What's more, Rob didn't even bother to apologize.

We got another booking – a proper one this time, as Joss gloatingly pointed out. The subject of songwriting had not been raised again. Rob had put one of his melodies down on cassette and I'd taken it to Kate, who had written some really nice words to it, which even Pip and Joss admitted were good. The song was called *Starchild* and was all about computers and space-age things. It was highly poetic, but we decided that it didn't matter if the audience didn't understand all the symbolism. 'Who understood Bob Dylan in his day?' Rob observed.

'Did you know that in some of the American univer-sities music students are writing theses about his songs now?' I informed him, glad to know something that he didn't. 'Maybe one day students will be studying Zero, instead of getting zero as their marks!'

Zero had been asked to play at the university. They often had groups performing there at weekends – we had been to hear quite a few, but had never guessed that one day we would be up there on stage, instead of in the audience.

'You know, we really ought to get some posters done,' I suggested.

'And how about tee-shirts?' Ireka put in.

'Hold on, hold on.' Joss was grinning as she held her hands up to shush us. 'Where's the money going to come from for all this?'

'Posters wouldn't cost much. We can get some large sheets of paper and do all the lettering ourselves,' Pip said. She got out her college notebook and began to play around with our name, Zero, and came up with a circle with a diagonal Z crossing it and the name of the group written in the middle.

'*When* we can afford tee-shirts –' Joss gave us all a stern look '– then we can use this symbol. We can have it on badges, too. What do you think?'

We were unanimous in our agreement.

Ever since the famous songwriting argument, I had stopped asking Rob for a go on his guitar, and I was quite missing it. Usually, after we'd run through the songs we were practising, he and I would spend fifteen minutes or so with the electric guitar while the others made coffee, tidied their things up and generally nattered around us. Today, though, the atmosphere among us all was so cheerful that I plucked up courage to mention it.

'Of course! But I thought you'd gone off the idea,' he said.

'It was after the argument,' I began, but he stopped me with, 'What argument? What are you talking about?'

'The — the day you said none of us could write songs,' I stammered.

'That wasn't an argument — that was a friendly discussion.' He chuckled. 'Argument, indeed. I hope you'll never be around when I have a *real* argument with anyone. Not that I lose my temper easily . . . except with my brother Andy. He and I have had some amazing fights. When we were younger, my mum only just stopped us from murdering each other on several occasions.'

'I'm glad you didn't succeed,' I murmured, then bit my lip.

'So am I — or else I wouldn't be here now . . .' I froze, held my breath. What was he about to say? *Here now, talking to the girl I love*? No, that was ridiculous. It was utterly far-fetched and impossible, I chided myself. And it must have been, too, because he finished his sentence with, '. . . playing in an about-to-be-famous rock band.'

Oh well, I thought. But for an instant my hopes had been re-kindled, and now I knew I was in for several hours, if not days, of self-torture, lying in bed thinking about him, unable to sleep, imagining scenes between us, impossible things like Zero getting to number one in the charts, and Rob asking me to marry him. Dreams – impossible, stupid, wonderful dreams.

Our concert at the university was received remarkably well. We could play for only three-quarters of an hour, because we didn't have enough material for longer, but we tried out Kate's new song, *Starchild*, and she and Dave sat in the audience, listening, enraptured. I had scanned the faces until I found them; I sang it to them, and they clutched each other's hands and it brought a lump of emotion and envy to my throat.

It was that night that we first realized that male groupies existed! It was our pretty Jamaican drummer who got all the attention. Four boys came up to us afterwards and, on the pretext of chatting to Ireka about drumming, asked her for dates.

She was tickled to death about it. 'Lloyd would go mad!' she shrieked, after she'd got rid of her admirers.

'What would I go mad about?' said a deep voice, and at that precise moment Lloyd, a six-foot-four, hulking Welsh rugby player, came striding into our untidy dressing-room. No-one told him, of course. He could have laid all four of Ireka's groupies flat with one smash of his ham-like fist!

'Who wants to go for a Chinese?' Lloyd enquired.

The rest of us shook our heads and so they went off together. Just as they'd disappeared, a middle-aged bloke tapped timidly at the door and poked his head round the doorframe. 'Everybody decent?' he asked.

His next question really threw us. 'Who's your manager?'

Chapter Eight

My first excited thought was that this guy of about forty, in a leather jacket and jeans, must be from a record company. He was about to offer us a recording contract – yes, that was it! I'd heard of this happening. Unknowns were suddenly 'discovered' and, after that, fame and fortune followed fast.

But it wasn't to be; not yet.

'My name's John Hamers. I work for an agency responsible for booking acts into hotels and clubs. I spend half my evenings popping along to gigs to see if there are any promising newcomers. You lot... you're a bit raw, but the punters like girls in a band. Now, if you could tart yourselves up a bit – you know, tight dresses, nice plunging tops –'

'Either our music's good enough without all that rubbish, or it isn't,' Joss snapped in frosty tones.

I felt a sudden stab of foreboding. If Joss was going to allow her feminist beliefs to come before our musical career, then I could see we wouldn't get very far. Surely, at this stage, we needed to take everything we were offered, both for the experience and the money?

The man shrugged, said, 'Well, it's your decision,' and was about to leave when I spoke up.

'Just a minute . . . give us a moment to talk this over, could you?'

'There's nothing to talk over,' Joss said threateningly.

It was about time I stood up to her, I decided. Obviously Rob wasn't going to say anything, and Pip would certainly back Joss up.

The man sidled out into the corridor, and I went over and shut the door. 'He's offering us work and we can't turn it down,' I stated emphatically. 'Anyway, lots of people make an effort to look good when they're on stage or TV. Why shouldn't we? It wouldn't hurt us, would it, just for one night?'

'Don't you understand anything?' Pip exploded. 'I think it's time we educated her,' she said to Joss. 'Where have you been for the last few years? Reading Barbara Cartland romances? We women have been fighting for years not to be looked on as sex objects, and to be accepted on equal terms with men, and here you are, trying to turn the clock back to the bad old days. You'll be telling me in a minute that you think women should be slaves to their husbands, and spend all day at the hairdresser's and the beauty parlour, and never read anything more improving than *Woman and Home*!'

Now she'd really made me angry. I wasn't going to let myself be insulted and talked down to like this! 'I know perfectly well what women's lib is all about and I agree with it wholeheartedly. But getting somewhere in life is a matter of compromise and tactics, not just following your beliefs blindly,' I said heatedly. 'I think you and Joss should swallow your pride, just for one night. *I'm* prepared to do it —'

'And I'm willing to wear false eyelashes and a frock if it would help,' Rob said, and I had to choke back a chuckle.

'Look at it this way. If, at this early stage, we're not prepared to take risks, or bend a bit to what people want, then we might as well split up now, because I certainly can't see any point in carrying on.'

'Shona has got a point . . .'

I gave Rob a grateful look.

'Oh well . . . maybe for just one night, but only if the money's good enough. And I am *not* going to wear something revealing so that men will ogle my tits,' Pip snorted.

'It's you who'll have to bear the brunt of it – you're our "front person",' Joss told me gruffly. I could tell she hated being beaten.

We called Mr Hamers back in and said we would do it. Our fee for one show was to be fifty pounds – ten pounds each, minus petrol money. It sounded like riches to me. Two bookings like this each week would more than pay my rent . . .

If I'd expected a glamorous nightclub, one look at the exterior of *Styles* was enough to disillusion me fast. The street the club was in looked so run down it was almost derelict, and the front door was almost indistinguishable from the shabby brickwork it was set in, covered in faded, peeling posters, soot and graffiti.

Repeated hammerings on the door produced a short, bald man, as wide as he was high, wearing shabby black trousers and a shirt which had come unbuttoned at the middle. He conducted us to our 'dressing-room', a cupboard which smelt abominably of greasy food.

'If it's any consolation,' Rob informed us, 'the Beatles used to play at places like this. So don't feel too down about it.'

'It'll probably turn out to be a strip joint,' Joss said gloomily.

'Yeah, *we'll* probably be expected to strip. Instead of clapping between numbers, they'll be yelling "gerr'em off!"' Pip prophesied grimly.

We decanted our instruments out of the van and lugged them down the dim, grimy corridor. The fat man, who was still hovering about, said he would show us the stage so we could set up our gear. It was tiny, and the red velvet curtain which divided it from the audience was so threadbare, it was almost see-through.

When we saw the house amplification system, our hearts sank still further.

'They'll be able to hear the drums and nothing else,' Ireka wailed.

'Oh, to be able to afford our own amplifiers!' Joss sighed.

We rigged up our instruments, had a quick practice which sounded dreadful and then went out to see what the area could offer us by way of food. We found a typical greasy spoon café complete with scratched, formica-topped tables, covered in brown and red rings from the sauce bottles and drips of other people's tea and coffee. After consuming some toasted sandwiches we left, the smell of rancid cooking fat clinging to our clothes as we made our way back to *Styles* for our ten o'clock appearance.

Before we went on, we peered out at the audience from the side of the stage. They were mostly men, clustered round tables and drinking beer amidst loud clinkings and deep bellows of laughter. It was the scariest-looking audience I'd seen to date. We had nothing in common with them, unlike the groups of friends, locals and fellow students we'd played to before.

'We'll be booed off within five minutes,' I moaned despairingly.

'I think we can write this one off right now,' Pip agreed.

'What? And lose fifty quid? Get out there, girl, and do your stuff!' Ireka urged, and Rob clapped her on the back, making her cough, and commented, 'That's the spirit!'

The fat gnome whom we'd imagined to be the doorman had turned out to be the club's manager.

'Time to go on, girls,' he insisted agitatedly. 'Now, you *are* going to play things everybody knows, aren't you? The boys do like a sing-along. Let's have *Tie A Yellow Ribbon Round the Old Oak Tree . . .*' He started to sing it. We all winced, especially Rob who took exception to being called a girl!

We walked out on stage and the audience scarcely interrupted their conversations to spare us a glance. The air was thick with cigarette and cigar smoke and I could feel it catching my throat as I began to sing. I soon realized we were fighting a losing battle. They didn't want to know. They went on making a row and we could hardly hear ourselves over the din.

I started to introduce our next number rather feebly, and suddenly Joss had leapt to my side and was grabbing the microphone.

'All right, all *right*!' she yelled. That made a few

heads turn. 'Now, we want you all to have a good time. We're going to do the old Beatles hit, *Twist and Shout* – there must be a few of you here who are old enough to remember that?'

To my surprise, there were a few chuckles.

'You're going to be our backing singers, right? I said *right*?' she repeated, and a chorus of *'rights'* came back. The audience were even beginning to put down their drinks and look interested.

'But we haven't even practised this one . . .' I hissed agitatedly to Pip.

'We'll muddle through. We have messed about with it a few times,' she said, but she was looking anxious, too.

'Now her over there on the drums is Ireka – show 'em, girl!' Joss screeched, and Ireka obligingly beat out a roll on her drum kit, earning a few cheers and ribald remarks, which made my blood boil. Gosh, they were a hideous lot!

'That's Pip on the bass – ' Pip plonked out a few notes and grinned. 'Rob's on guitar – ' He got a few whistles and remarks about how lucky he was. 'I'm Joss on the keyboard and our singer is the scintillating Shona Patterson. Right, kids – a-one, two, three.'

She darted back behind her synthesizer as Ireka, Rob and Pip started up rather raggedly. I almost forgot where to come in, but it didn't matter – the audience had already started. And it was like that for the rest of our turn. We bashed out the oldies, no matter how badly, and the audience loved it. And – which was weird – I enjoyed it, too, loving the feedback of good humour and energy, even if it was accompanied by the rhythmic bashing of pint glasses on wooden table-tops!

'*Phew*!' I gasped as we ran off stage to a chorus of cheers and requests for more. 'I'm absolutely dripping!'

'Look at me,' Ireka groaned, and pretended to wring out her tee-shirt.

We dried ourselves off – no luxuries like showers in this place – and packed up our things, then went in search of the manager so that we could get our money.

He fished in his pocket and withdrew a roll of bank-notes, peeled off several fivers and handed them to Pip. She was about to pocket them when Rob reminded her that she ought to count them. Forty pounds! She counted them again, to make sure, but there were only eight notes there.

Rob took charge. 'We were promised by John Hamers that the fee for tonight was to be fifty pounds,' he said firmly.

'That's right.' The portly little man stood his ground.

'Well, where's the other tenner?'

'Commission. All agencies take commission, didn't you know? Twenty per cent's the going rate. I've taken it out of your money and I'll pass it on to John.'

'None of this was explained to us,' Rob said threat-eningly. I could see his fists clenching and unclenching.

'Let's take it and get out of here,' Joss ground out furiously.

All the way home in the van we grumbled about the injustice of it. We all agreed that, in future, if we didn't already know the people we were going to be playing for, we would sort everything out properly beforehand, so that nothing like this ever happened again.

I was almost nodding off during the journey home when Joss suddenly gave a shriek. 'My God – it's that shorthand test tomorrow!'

'Oh *no*!' I gasped. Like her, I'd completely forgotten about it. It was all right for Pip and Ireka, as they were doing another course and presumably had their tests at different times from us. But I hadn't done a stroke of work and I knew Joss hadn't, either.

'How tired are you, Shona?' she asked me.

'Absolutely shattered,' I replied truthfully.

'Mmm. So am I. But there's just one thing that might work, if we can prop our eyelids open for another couple of hours. Spend the night at my place and we'll test each other and correct each other's work. It's the only thing I can think of.'

I couldn't think of anything I wanted to do less than work when all my instincts told me to seek a nice soft pillow and a dreamless sleep. But I knew that my work had been suffering since we had started with Zero and, most reluctantly, I agreed. We dropped Ireka off, then Rob, then Pip dropped us off and I followed Joss up her millions of stairs with aching legs and a feeling of acute depression. I didn't want to get thrown out of college. It was my only chance of eventually getting a job – and besides, I couldn't bear to upset my parents. But I didn't want to give Zero up, even if it meant working until 3 a.m.

Joss made some strong black coffee and got out the biscuit tin. 'Sit down,' she said, groaning as she eased her own tired limbs into a cross-legged position on the floor. 'This is going to be a long, hard night . . .'

Chapter Nine

The last-minute cramming paid off because we both got through the test better than we had expected. My whole body felt bruised and aching from having had four hours of heavy sleep on Joss's lumpy sofa and I was looking forward to a night in my own comfy bed, but Fate had other things up its sleeve, in the shape of a frantic message from Pip. Some guy she knew had phoned to say a band had let his mate down, and could Zero substitute at the eleventh hour. Pip had, of course, said yes.

'It's all right for her,' I grumbled to Joss. 'She hasn't had a test today.'

'Yes, I know what you mean,' Joss groaned, rubbing her strained, tired eyes. She looked dreadful, and I knew I must, too. We went to find Ireka, who was as bouncy and full of beans as usual. Then we tracked down Rob in the basement laboratory.

Pip's contact was attached to a theatre company, and the show we were playing in was being staged at an arty little theatre, with a bar, club and small gallery all in the same building. We had to supply half an hour of entertainment, which was quite easy, and after we'd finished we went for a drink in the bar. To our surprise, we found someone else was footing the bill – a large, square woman with wild hair dyed a vivid magenta colour. She was wearing baggy white trousers and an overshirt covered in brilliant, multi-coloured streaks and splotches.

She greeted us with a beaming smile and a wave of a be-ringed hand. 'Hi. I'm Fleur Jacowski.' She paused, as if waiting for us to recognize her name, but none of us did, so she went on: 'I liked your show. You've got a lot of talent. In the right hands you could be really good. But right now you lack direction. You need someone to pull you together, give you an image –'

'That's what we've been saying to ourselves,' gabbled Ireka, and Pip and Joss glared at her. Who *was* this woman? I felt instinctively suspicious of her, partly because she looked so well-off.

'I know a lot about putting on shows. I've been an actress, I've produced and directed, and right now I'm in theatrical management; several of my clients are dancers and singers. I think I could do something with you, but we'd need to sit down and have a serious talk. How about ten o'clock tomorrow morning, at my office in Bold Street? Here's my card.' She dived into her embroidered suede handbag, produced a white card with gold embossed lettering on it and handed it to Ireka.

'See you tomorrow, then,' she stated, as if it was all settled.

'I'm sorry, but we won't be able to make it then,' Ireka informed her. 'We've got classes all day to-morrow.'

Fleur Jacowski frowned. 'Somehow I'd never have guessed you were students. I thought you were full-time musicians. This does put a new light on things. However, I'm sure we can overcome any problems,' she said cheerfully.

'Maybe we could miss that lecture on Office Procedure,' Joss muttered to me. 'It sounds phenomenally boring, and we could borrow someone else's notes later . . .'

Ireka said she could probably give her class a miss as well, and Pip said she didn't have anything till eleven, anyway.

'I definitely can't make it,' Rob said distractedly. 'There's going to be a demonstration of something really important. If I miss it, I'll never be able to understand it. There's some science bod from the university coming over specially.'

Our potential link with success couldn't hear this hasty discussion as she was busy exchanging loud small-talk with some acquaintance of hers who had just walked in. When we next had her attention, we told her that four-fifths of Zero would be able to make the appointment, and she looked pleased. I was certainly very excited about it. If she was involved in the theatre, she just had to know loads of people . . .

We met by St Luke's Church next morning and strolled down Bold Street, looking in shop windows and searching for numbers on doors. Then we found it, a green-painted door at the side of a shop which sold greetings cards and art reproductions.

It was a third-floor walk-up and the stairs were

narrow, dark and creaky.

'Bit seedy, isn't it? I don't know if I could trust anybody who worked from a place like this,' I remarked suspiciously.

We got to the top of the stairs and paused soberly for a while before the door marked *Fleur Jacowski, Theatrical Management*. I felt a twinge of excitement once we got inside. Where the other parts of the building were seedy, Fleur's offices were designed and furnished in a bright, modern style, with lots of strong colours, glass and tubular steel.

The girl at the reception desk asked who we were, then buzzed through to Fleur's room. Seconds later Fleur herself bounded out to meet us.

'Great . . . great. Glad you could make it. I've been doing lots of thinking. The boy . . . Where is he? Not here? That's good. Come in, come in.'

I was mystified. Why should Rob's absence be good? He was the best instrumentalist of the lot of us.

The four of us crammed into her small office, Pip perching herself on the corner of the desk. As Fleur unfolded her masterplan, I listened with interest at first, but then with a growing sense of indignation which I could see wasn't shared by at least two of our members.

'. . . So I think,' she concluded, 'that Zero would be far better off as an all-female outfit. Let's face it, feminism's in the news. Bands with boys in are two a penny, but good all-girl groups with a strong female message can't help but attract the media. You'll see.'

She didn't ask us to sign on the dotted line, for which I was thankful, because I didn't want us to get involved in an argument here, in her office. I didn't even bother to say goodbye to Fleur, and the moment we were out on the stairs again, I exploded.

'The woman's mad! Of *course* we can't get rid of Rob. We need a guitarist. And anyway, he's the only one of us who can write good melodies.' Joss glared at me, but I carried on, undaunted. 'And we need him for other things, too. He's . . . well, he's . . .' I found they were things I couldn't put into words. He was cheerful and reassuring and strong. He was a shoulder to cry on. He was a chaperon, protecting us from predatory males. He was . . .

I suddenly realized that it was probably only me who saw him like this. He meant so much to me personally. The only arguments that would make sense to the group were the musical ones. But there were loads more reasons why *I* couldn't do without him. If he was kicked out, I wouldn't want to stay. They could find another singer.

But wouldn't I be making myself look a fool if I quit? As far as the others were concerned, Rob and I meant nothing to each other – and, I thought dolefully, as far as Rob was concerned, too. I'd be throwing away our big chance – for what? It wouldn't make Rob fall in love with me, would it?

We got to the bottom of the gloomy stairs and out into the brightness of the street and I blinked, not just because of the strong light but because my eyes were misty with tears.

'Who's going to tell him, because I'm certainly not,' I announced savagely. I felt like kicking something, or some*body*, I was so confused. When you're in love

56

with someone who doesn't love you, just having them near can be some consolation, because then you can dream and imagine and hope that, one day, it might all change. If Rob went, the last link with him would be taken away from me and life would be unbearable.

'I'm going home,' I said. 'I need to think about all this. Joss, be a mate and tell them I'm ill or something, will you? I'll see you lot tomorrow.'

I'd meant to use my illegal day off swotting and catching up with my work. I had an essay to do – no, *two* – and I was way behind with my shorthand. Thank heaven it was only the Spring term. Next term was when the big exams happened. Zero would have to cool its musical career then, anyway, so I'd only have lost Rob in the long run. Perhaps it was better for it to happen sooner rather than later, when I might have been even more crazy about him. Fancy suffering from unrequited love at seventeen, I rebuked myself. By now I should be over things like this, I should be mature and adult and able to control my emotions, shouldn't I?

I sank down on the side of my bed and rested my head in my hands. Seventeen – and oh, so green. That rhymed, I realized hollowly. So what? *When I was seventeen, didn't know I was so green* . . . I picked up a pen from the bedside table and scribbled the lines down in my notebook. Maybe they would come in useful for something. Not now, though; I was far too miserable to feel creative.

Next day, I walked up the steps to the college entrance with dragging feet and my heart feeling like one of those solid iron cannonballs you see in museums, weighing me down to the ground. To my surprise, when I got into the lecture room Joss didn't look any happier. I'd no sooner started talking to Kate and telling her about it than Joss interrupted us.

'Sorry, Kate, but I must talk to Shona before your lecture starts. Look, Shona, I don't want you thinking Pip and I are rejoicing about this. We don't like it any more than you do. Of course Rob's good – he's brilliant. He adds an awful lot to the band. But we do need an image and an identity if the public are going to remember us. We've already got those funny anti-men songs, and that one Pip got from her women's action group. I feel that we're going that way even though we don't realize it. Perhaps it's Fate . . .'

She pulled a wry face. 'Anyway, Pip's left a note in Rob's pigeon-hole telling him there's a rehearsal tonight. We'll talk it all over then, okay?'

I wanted to rush off immediately and warn him. I couldn't bear to think of him going through the day in ignorance of what was going to happen to him tonight. But I needn't have worried as, when the moment came and Joss broke the news, he seemed quite prepared for it.

'I could tell she was a man-hater. Didn't even look at me,' he said. His mouth was set in a thin line and my heart was breaking. 'There's really no point in my staying, is there? I'll go now,' he decided, picking up his guitar case and pushing open Joss's blue door.

'No! Rob . . .' The words flew from my mouth and I couldn't control them, although everyone else was staring at me. I bit my lip, looked down at the ground and mumbled, 'It's all right. It's nothing.'

'Okay. See you around, folks. It was good while it lasted,' he said bitterly, while I choked back my tears.

I heard the slam of the door and the thudding of his feet on the stairs – and when I next looked up, the room was empty. Oh, I know all the others were in it, but *for me* it was empty, because Rob wasn't there. I heard myself agreeing mechanically to get an electric guitar – 'You were getting really good with Rob teaching you. You'll soon be as good as him,' I was assured – and practise hard and write more songs and rehearse even harder. I even agreed that we should phone Fleur in the morning and let her know that she could manage us.

Then I was free – free to go home and sit in my room and see nothing but Rob's face, with that scornful, hurt look in his eyes. *He* knew Zero would never make it without him, I thought. Good grief, *I* wasn't going to be able to make it without him! What was the point in going on living from day to day if there wasn't that promise of seeing him nearly every night at rehearsals? I felt like ringing up my parents and telling them I was quitting college and coming home.

I knew I was going crazy and needed someone to talk to, so I went round to Kate's, but she had Dave there so that was no good. I had a cup of coffee with them then went home again – and all at once those words I'd scribbled on the pad leapt out at me, and more started to form. *How my heart was torn and twisted – he didn't know that I existed . . .* God, it was so true. I was half sobbing as I wrote it down.

It took me hours. I didn't know if it was any good or

not, but by the next morning I had a complete song there – well, the words, at least; every one torn from my heart. I'd tried hard to make it applicable to other people as well as myself. I called it *Chapters* and it was about stages in one's life. It was an expression of bitterness and disillusionment. *He's just another chapter in the book I'm going to write, Someday when I've got the time and life ain't such a fight . . . I'll tell the story of another love in vain, Another ghost to howl around the alleys of my brain – If I can remember his name . . .*

I tore the sheets of paper from my pad and stuffed them out of sight in a drawer. I couldn't show this to anyone – not yet. Rob, I sighed. Oh, Rob . . . When will I ever see you again . . .?

Chapter Ten

It felt as if music was my whole life now and everything else – studies, social activities, even my parents – took a back seat. I would have to pay a visit home soon as my birthday was coming up and I knew my parents would want to celebrate and give me presents, as it was my eighteenth.

My birthday was on a Wednesday and so I promised to go home the following Saturday, just for the day, so that Mum and Dad could see I was still alive. They had sounded very suspicious of all my excuses for not seeing them and I was convinced they thought that I was having a passionate affair with someone. If only . . .

I decided to ask all my friends if they would like to come to a Chinese restaurant with me, but when I asked Ireka and told her where I planned on going, she looked really sad and wistful.

'Lloyd and I used to go there sometimes . . .' she said.

'What do you mean, used to?'

'Oh, Shona . . .' It was the first time I'd seen her depressed. She was usually so bright and bubbly no matter what happened. 'I suppose I'll have to tell everyone sooner or later, it's not the sort of thing you can keep secret for long,' she said sadly. 'And I suppose it's my fault really, not spending enough time with him. You see, he's found someone else.'

'Oh, no!' I gasped, shocked and sympathetic. 'Who?'

'I don't know. I don't *want* to know, I'd probably kill her if I did. Some nurse . . . He didn't even tell me. I found out from one of his mates.' She sighed heavily and I patted her shoulder.

'If he could do a thing like that, he's not worth eating your heart out over,' I insisted, thinking that maybe Joss had a bit of a point and most men *were* rotters.

'I suppose you're right,' Ireka agreed glumly.

'Look, you come out with us on Wednesday and we'll go somewhere else. Do come. It might cheer you up a bit.'

She did come in the end and we went for a curry at an

Indian place instead. There were eleven of us, including Keith Randall and Mike Broadway, whom we'd bumped into in the pub. I'd asked Rob but he'd told me very apologetically that he couldn't make it as he had an important test on Thursday and he would need Wednesday night to revise as, in common with the rest of us, he hadn't been studying very hard lately. My heart had sunk right down into my boots, but I knew I couldn't let it show and that I would have to brazen out my birthday celebration as if nothing at all was wrong.

In the end, we had a jolly good evening, with Keith and Mike on top joke-cracking form. It was nearly midnight by the time we all spilled out onto the pavement and shivered in the freezing February air. I was heartily glad of the matching scarf and gloves that Kate had given me.

When I got home, I found that the post had arrived after I'd left that morning and I had several more cards and gifts to open. One thing that pleased me was that all my relatives had sent me money, which I intended putting straight into the electric guitar fund.

I ripped the envelopes open greedily, read the greetings inside, then propped the cards up on the mantelpiece. So, when I came to a long, pale green envelope, I treated it no differently to all the rest. The card had a lovely Chinese picture of butterflies on it which I studied pleasurably for a few seconds before opening it to see who it was from. The name of the sender leapt off the page at me. *Rob*!

Congratulations on reaching 18. Hope you have a really fabulous day and sorry I couldn't be there to enjoy it with you. Love, Rob. My heart pounded as I read and re-read the message. There was no stamp on the envelope so either he had come round with it personally or had given it to Kate to put through the door.

I hugged the card to me and almost kissed it, I was so completely thrilled. Ever since Rob had stopped coming to rehearsals I had felt half alive and knew I wasn't singing and playing as well as I used to, when he was my chief inspiration. I hardly ever saw him at college, either. Maybe he was keeping out of Zero's way because he was so cheesed off at being kicked out. Yet just because he despised Joss didn't mean he had to hate me, too.

I sighed, and studied the message in the card again. He'd only put *love*, I noted, not even *lots of love*. But then, what did I expect? I was wishing for the moon as usual . . .

I placed the card on the mantelpiece with the others and sat for a while, thinking that, if it wasn't for him, I'd have had a really happy birthday. To torture myself still more, I found the words to my song, *Chapters*, and read them over and over until I was almost in tears. Then I put them back in the drawer and forced myself to snap out of my misery by counting the money I'd been given. It came to nearly forty pounds and if I could get twenty more from somewhere, I'd be able to buy the second-hand electric guitar I'd seen in the window of a music shop in town. Though, knowing my luck, by the time I had enough cash it would have been sold.

In that respect at least, Fate smiled kindly on me. When I paid my visit home that Saturday, Dad gave me a fat cheque to spend on anything I wanted – so at lunchtime on Monday, I walked out of the shop feeling ten miles high, a professional rock guitarist at last!

Mike Broadway kindly provided me with a small practice amp which he had bought once when attempting to learn the guitar, only to give up when he found the piano was better for composing on. I bought a Teach Yourself cassette like the one Rob had, and set about practising every available moment.

Fleur was not turning out to be a very good manager. In five weeks, she only managed to get us two bookings, one in a theatre club and one in a hotel. We had followed her advice and adopted a kind of uniform of baggy shirts and trousers, which we hand-painted ourselves with fabric paint. It was great fun doing that. Joss said she didn't *really* mind getting paint all over her carpet, though we did our best to scrub it off with turpentine.

One annoying thing about Fleur was that she flew off the handle easily. I had written a new song, ideal for Zero, called *The Perfect Man*, which Joss had set to music for me. Fleur was the only one who didn't think it was funny. In it, I described the ideal man as sensitive, intelligent, witty and house-trained, a good lover, a brilliant cook; *Doing something quite nouvelle with kiwi fruit and pears, Whilst painting his next masterpiece and hoovering the stairs*. It ended with the lament that you could never find one of these paragons because they had all been snapped up by perfect girls before you got a chance to lay your hands on one.

Fleur objected to that sentiment. 'It's sexist, dearie. You *are* the perfect girl – we all are. Your song gives the impression that men still go for empty-headed dolls with perfect figures . . .'

'That's not what I'm saying at all,' I broke in.

'Well, that's what it sounds like, lovey. It's not Zero. Just change that last verse.'

'No I bloody well won't,' I muttered mutinously as we left that particular meeting. The others couldn't understand Fleur either, but the upshot was that she wouldn't let us perform the song. I was furious.

Then we got a booking ourselves, through Mike Broadway, at a teachers' training college on the Lancashire coast. It was the first out-of-town gig we had ever done, and we were understandably excited about it. We couldn't believe it when we told Fleur and she informed us that, as our manager, she was entitled to ten per cent of our fee for the night!

'But it's going to cost us a packet to get there!' screamed Joss. 'Anyway, I got that booking myself, through my cousin. You didn't have anything to do with it.'

'That's hardly the point,' Fleur replied frostily, irritatingly tapping her ballpoint on the glass desk top. 'We're all in this together, you know.'

'Yes, and a fat lot you're doing,' I couldn't resist adding.

Fleur clapped her hands over her ears. 'Girls . . . ladies . . . stop it, please! An artiste and his or her manager . . . it's like a marriage, don't you see? You've got to give it time to mature and develop. Each side has got to put in an equal amount.'

Pip, who had been reading an article in a music paper about managers, said, 'Most managers are prepared to put something in financially at the beginning. You should at least buy us some decent amplifiers, and maybe a van.'

'Yes, and organize us a roadie to help with our equipment,' added Joss. 'You can get female ones, you know. My friend Jacky—'

'I am doing my level best to help you lot, and this is all the thanks I get . . . Who are you? Nobody. Listen to some of the people I deal with all day . . .' Fleur proceeded to reel off a list of names we had never heard of. Well, hardly ever. Those that were vaguely familiar were ancient and past it. It was glaringly obvious that Fleur was not right for us.

'She's not getting a penny of our money for Saturday,' spat Joss, as we trudged down the stairs from her office, our lunch break nearly over.

'Too right!' chirped Ireka, and Pip and I agreed.

But Saturday night was to prove eventful, in more ways than one . . .

Chapter Eleven

Out of the corner of my eye, I could see Pip gesturing at me, but I couldn't tell what she was on about because we were in the middle of a song. But in between numbers she came scooting over. 'The guitar's not sounding right,' she hissed in my ear. 'Try twiddling some knobs or something.'

'I can't!' I wailed. 'I don't know what to do.'

In the middle of this, Ireka was already tapping out the introductory rhythms to the next song, and I launched into it half-heartedly. It was difficult enough playing my new guitar, without having to sing as well — and to know that it wasn't sounding right was a real downer. Oh God, I thought dementedly, why wasn't Rob here? Why had we listened to that stupid woman? How much happier I would have been, and how much better I would be singing, if only he were here . . .

We limped to the end of the gig somehow and, to our amazement, got called back for an encore, but my heart wasn't in it.

'What the hell was the matter with you tonight?' Pip snapped crossly, the moment we got back to our dressing room.

'Oh, leave her — she's probably got the curse or something. Have you, Shona?' Joss said. I was surprised that she seemed to be on my side for once. I could have lied and appealed to their sympathy, but I didn't. I just slammed that rotten electric guitar down on the bench.

'It's this thing,' I muttered savagely. 'I could smash it to pieces . . .'

'That would be great in the act! Why don't you?'

The intruding male voice came from the direction of the door.

'Go away!' Ireka shrieked. She was right in the middle of changing from her sweaty tee-shirt to a jumper.

But the bloke showed no signs of budging. 'I'd like a

word with you, please. Have you got a recording contract?' he said unexpectedly.

'Fat chance,' Joss sneered.

'I'm serious,' he protested. He was lean and curly-haired and dressed in the latest style of jeans and matching canvas jacket. A real Mr Cool.

'Have you signed a management contract?' he persisted.

'No, thank God,' I snorted, thinking of the useless Fleur.

'Better and better! Look, I'd better introduce myself. I'm Mel Katz.'

'What?' Our four heads jerked in unison as we looked him up and down. We'd actually heard of him. He managed Cycle Tour, a new band from Manchester who had just had their first hit record. My heart began to race. We had thought our big break was imminent that night we met Fleur, but we'd been wrong. It was now – this was it! *And* – and this thought made me feel almost faint with excitement and elation – being a bloke, he might not object if Rob came back and joined us!

An hour and a pizza apiece later, Mel knew all about us, and we knew a fair bit about him. He scoffed at the idea of our being managed by a Theatrical Agent. 'You'd have ended up at some crummy seaside town doing a summer season with some clapped-out comic who was famous twenty years ago,' he said. 'Now, my plan is to book a demo studio and get your best numbers down on tape. Then I'll get an arranger along and –'

'Hey, I don't know about an arranger. All this is

going a bit fast for me,' Ireka complained.

'I know what I'm doing.' Mel shot her a sharp look.

'Okay, okay.' Ireka bowed to his greater musical knowledge.

When we got back, although it was after one in the morning, I was filled with a wicked urge to go round to Rob's and tell him what had happened. I couldn't help it, it wasn't just because I was – no, not *in love,* I refused to use that term – *so fond* of him, but because, to me, he still felt as if he were part of the band. Pip dropped me off at the end of my road and the old van rattled and coughed off into the night, but I didn't walk down the street. Instead, I stood and took two or three deep, gusty breaths of the delicious, cold night air and then started walking.

'I must be mad,' I thought when I was over halfway there. 'I must be well and truly bonkers.'

It took me over half an hour to get to his house and as I stood outside, staring up at those dark, curtained windows, the enthusiasm ebbed out of me as if I'd been a carton of orange juice that had sprung a leak. I felt drained, empty and easily crushable. Which window was Rob's? How could I attract his attention? He'd be fast asleep.

The moon glimpsed out through a tear in a scudding cloud and I shivered as the wind whipped icy fingers round my face, neck and ankles. What if he should look out of the window now and see me? What would he think – that I was standing here in love-sick worship, keeping some kind of crazy vigil, or spying on him or something?

But now that I had come all this way, I had to do

something. I couldn't ring the doorbell at this time of night. Making a decision, I pushed open the front gate, bent and scrabbled around in the border and came up with a handful of small stones. I took careful aim and pitched one at the window, then waited, my throat dry with nerves. Nothing happened. I hurled another, larger one. Still nothing. I examined the others I held, but there was nothing that wouldn't risk breaking the glass. Disconsolately, I let them drop onto the pavement. Then, cold and tired, I started the long walk back . . .

My thoughts must have reached him, though, because next morning I was just plodding my weary way through the reception area towards the main staircase when a hand suddenly shot across in front of me.

'Halt, who goes there? Name me a number less than one!'

'Rob!' I stared at him disbelievingly, my stomach giving a kind of lurch when I took in how wonderful he looked. He'd had his hair cut, it was shorter and it suited him. How glad I was now that he hadn't known I was outside his house the previous night. I'd narrowly escaped being labelled a total loony.

'How goes it? Haven't seen you for ages. Thought maybe you'd made the Top Ten and left.' He grinned and I suddenly felt as if all the scores of people scurrying around us weren't really there but were projections on a cinema screen and only Rob and I were real. Shapes and colours went flickering past, but Rob and I were alone by the foot of the staircase and my typing lesson wasn't about to start yet.

'I've got an electric guitar, you know,' I said. It was

the only bit of news I could think of. Mel and last night had gone right out of my head.

'Why don't you bring it round this evening and let me have a look at it?'

My mouth dropped open and I had to make a physical effort to shut it, swallow, and nod. 'Yes . . . fine . . . I'd love to,' I stumbled. Then the sudden silence around us snapped me back to reality. We were late for our classes — everyone else would be already in their seats, notebooks out.

'You'll be in trouble,' I warned him. 'You'd better go.'

He grinned again and shrugged. 'See you later.' Then he was gone, leaping up the stairs, taking them three at a time, so that I was terrified he might trip and have a dreadful accident. But he didn't, of course.

After that, I didn't care about the rest of the day. Gina told me off and it was hard not to laugh. Kate wasn't in class, and that did worry me. As it was Friday, I wondered if maybe she had gone away for a long weekend – with Dave, perhaps. I promised myself that I'd call round at her place and check. It was ages since we'd had a decent gossip, anyway.

Joss wasn't pleased when I told her where I was going. She pulled a face. 'But we need to talk about Mel Katz and everything . . .'

'And I need to sort out my guitar. You heard it last night.'

We faced each other obstinately, and with a sigh she gave in. 'Tomorrow, then. Make it twelve-ish. I've got to go out before then, to try and find my sister's engagement present.'

Engagement present? I thought in amazement. So Joss's family weren't all like her, some did conventional things! I decided it was safer not to comment.

Walking into Rob's was almost like coming home, because it was the place where I'd wanted to be for so long. He must have been watching out for me because I could hear his footsteps thundering down the stairs just as I was moving my hand towards the bell.

His room was incredibly tidy and I felt sure it must be in my honour. There was even a vase containing some daffodils on a table by the window.

'Let's have a look at it then.'

I undid the metal clips of the solid, heavy electric guitar case and handed him my new instrument. He frowned slightly as he scrutinized it.

'How much did you pay for it?' he asked me.

'Sixty.'

'Not bad.' He plugged it into his amplifier, twiddled with the tuning knobs and strummed a few experimental chords. 'Slightly on the tinny side, but you can't expect perfection. It's got nice action, good and easy, though I might lower the bridge just a little for you. But these strings!' He screwed his face up in horror. 'What are they? Fuse wire?'

I felt really ashamed. I knew by now what I had done wrong, but I felt desperately embarrassed about having to admit it to him and have him thinking me even more of an idiot then he already supposed.

He began to chuckle. 'Go on, Shona, you must tell me.'

'Mandolin strings,' I admitted dolefully. 'The shop gave me the wrong ones and I didn't realize until I got

72

them home, and then I was so keen to play that I didn't want to have to wait till the next day when I could change them, and they've sort of been on there ever since . . .'

Rob threw his head back and hooted with laughter, rocking backward and catching his knees with his hands. 'Mandolin strings – that's classic!' he spluttered, and by now I was laughing, too. 'No wonder you were having trouble with the sound. Here –'

He took a box off his dressing table and rummaged around in it. 'I've got a spare set you can have. I'll put them on for you,' he offered.

'I'll pay you for them,' I began, but he wouldn't hear of it.

'So how's your playing now? I know it's bad of me but I haven't been to any of your concerts since I got the boot. I won't hide the fact that I was a bit hurt. Do you still want to borrow that Teach Yourself cassette I mentioned ages ago?'

'No thanks, I've bought one,' I informed him, hoping it didn't sound as if I was rejecting his offer deliberately.

'I should have lent it to you ages ago. So you've got a tape recorder, then?'

'I borrowed the one Kate's brother left behind,' I explained.

'Well, let's hear you, then.' Rob finished adjusting my new set of strings and plugged both our guitars into his amp, adding: 'It's okay, the landlord's out. Tonight's his car maintenance class, and they all go to the pub afterwards.'

We started playing one of Zero's songs and, just like

always, I was struck by how well our voices harmonized together, and how clever he was at weaving musical notes around the rather bare chords I was playing. We played for about half an hour, standing in the middle of his room, the floor and bed littered with manuscript paper and records which had certain tracks on that he had suggested I listen to for inspiration. I was just thinking that I had never, ever, enjoyed myself so much, when there was a ring at the doorbell, a pause, then another, more prolonged ring.

'Damn!' Rob swore, disentangling himself from his guitar strap. 'I'll just go and see who that is.'

Curious, I lurked in the doorway as he pounded down the stairs. I couldn't see into the hallway, but I could hear voices – Rob's surprised: 'Oh, hello . . .' and an answering female voice: 'You did say today, didn't you?'

Waves of heat and cold buffeted me as I clung to the doorframe. So Rob had a girlfriend . . . Why had I never thought of that? Why had I stupidly taken it for granted that he was sitting at home dreaming of me, just because I never ceased to think about him? He must have read it in my eyes – the idiotic, blind adoration, the excitement at being near him. How he must have been laughing to himself! I'd never felt so humiliated.

Anger brought a surge of energy and I rushed back into his room, crammed my guitar into its case, grabbed my shoulderbag and jacket and marched bravely down the stairs, my head held high even though I was blinking back tears. Rob and the short, dark-haired, pretty girl he was talking to, looked at me in amazement.

I shot my rival a sickly smile. 'Rob's been giving me a guitar lesson and I was just leaving,' I explained, trying to stop my voice from wavering.

The door was open and I walked through. ''Bye, Rob,' I said through gritted teeth.

'But Shona –' he began.

''Bye,' I repeated and, without looking back, I strode off down the road, gulping the bitter air of defeat.

Chapter Twelve

After that, I threw myself into Zero in earnest. Joss certainly could not have grumbled about any lack of dedication on my part now, which was just as well because Mel Katz was living up to his reputation as a hitmaker and was drilling us like troops. He had been quick to point out that my guitar-playing left a lot to be desired, and sent me off to take lessons from an ageing session guitarist who was brilliant and who improved my playing more in two weeks than three years of self-tuition had done. He gave me lots of useful – and necessary – tips, too, like how to strengthen my finger-nails with layers of clear varnish and thin tissue paper, so that they wouldn't break while I was playing, and hardening my fingertips with methylated spirits.

Mel paid for the lessons, which impressed us all as it meant he had to be serious about us. He also decided that we should all dress in Joss's army-gear look, because it drove home our 'big tough women' angle. He maintained that we looked really sexy in baggy khaki flying suits, and loads of belts strung round us.

'We don't want to look sexy,' Joss thundered, but Mel's instant reply was, 'You'll do as I say. Think of the money.'

True to his word, he got us into a recording studio and it was really exciting, waiting until the little red light came on, then singing into a microphone, unencumbered by a guitar because we had already recorded the backing track and it was being played to me through a set of headphones.

But when we crowded round the speakers to hear our efforts being played back, Mel shook his head. 'There isn't a single here,' he grumbled. 'Plenty of good album tracks, but no single. Haven't you got anything else?'

I agreed to call on Kate that evening, to see if she had written any more lyrics. I hadn't been at college for two days – none of the members of Zero had, as we'd been far too busy with our recording session. I was dying to tell Kate all about it, but one look at her face when she opened the door to me told me that – for a change – it was I who was going to have to do the listening.

'Oh Shona, it's so good to see you,' she said. Then her face sort of broke up and, with a gulp, she confessed, 'I've never been so miserable in my whole life. Dave . . . Dave's just f-finished with me!' With that, she flung herself at me and burst into floods of tears.

'Oh God . . . Oh, I am sorry, Kate.' I put an arm round her and led her back inside. 'Tell me about it.' I was feeling really guilty for not having been close to her over the past few weeks. If I had been around, perhaps I could have helped.

Her parents were out and she had been watching telly in the lounge. I went over and switched it off, and Kate raised tragic eyes to me.

'He – he rang, about twenty minutes ago. He said he didn't know how to tell me, but his ex-girlfriend, someone he'd known for years, had just said she wanted to go out with him again. Apparently, they broke up a few months ago after a big row, but he's . . .' She covered her face with her hands and I felt so helpless, just sitting by her, patting her shoulders and making soothing noises.

'He says he's still in love with her,' Kate finished in a whisper. 'I don't know who she is, or anything about her. I don't know whether she's beautiful – I don't even know if she's here in Liverpool. All I know is that I hate her . . . yet I shouldn't. Afer all, Dave was hers first.'

'And she let him go!' I reminded Kate savagely. 'She's got no right just to come wandering back into his life and ruin things for you.'

'But if he really does love her, I can't do anything about it. After all, he never said he loved me . . .' She broke down again.

'Please stop crying,' I begged her. 'He's not worth it. Look, I'll go and make us both a cup of tea, while you think of all the horrid things about him that you could never stand!'

'We were going to go away for Easter, too,' were the words that echoed after me as I went down the hall towards the kitchen . . .

Easter! I'd forgotten all about the approaching holiday. My parents would be expecting me to go home, I thought guiltily. As the crow flies, I wasn't all that far away from them – they were just a bit further up the river, on the other side. But to get there was a real hassle involving trains and buses, and I'd only seen them for one weekend and a few odd nights since Christmas, though I frequently spoke to them on the phone. They hadn't met Kate, though they knew of her as my particular friend at college.

'I've got an idea,' I told her. 'Why don't you come and stay with us for a bit? I'm sure Mum and Dad wouldn't mind, and I think you'd like them. If the weather stays nice like this, wouldn't it be great to go into the Welsh mountains for a picnic? There's this lovely little village in the Conway Valley where we used to stay for holidays when I was little . . .'

Kate's glum expression began to lighten. 'I haven't been to Wales for years,' she said. 'If your parents don't object, I'd love to come, to take my mind off the Dave business.'

'Do you mind if I call them on your phone? I'll keep it short,' I promised.

Two minutes later, I was able to tell her the holiday was on . . . but two days after that, it looked distinctly threatened.

I was still trying to keep all knowledge of Zero away from my parents as I knew I'd only get lectures about working for qualifications being more important than

78

having fun. If they only knew how little fun playing in a group was! And then Mel told us he'd got us a booking for Easter Monday at an open-air festival in Buckinghamshire. The promoters had organized it at the last minute, in the hope that the fine spell would hold, and were having difficulty finding bands who were free.

'It'll be a great chance for you to have some exposure in another part of the country. Good experience, too,' he said briskly, at a hasty lunch-time meeting. 'I'm afraid you're on in the morning, though. The more important the band, the later they play.'

'I suppose we're on at dawn then,' Ireka joked, with a slight edge to her voice. With the rest of us, she felt just slightly upset that, in the eyes of the world, Zero were way down at the bottom of the bill.

'Where's Joss?' I wondered suddenly. 'She wasn't in class this morning.'

'Oh, she's gone to some shop to see about a new microchip for her whatsit. Something's not sounding right in her keyboard,' Pip explained.

'Make sure you get her to the Phil tonight,' Mel ordered. 'I want to see you all about the rest of the arrangements, but I need to make some calls first.'

The Philharmonic pub, on the corner opposite the Philharmonic concert hall, was a large, cavernous building with ornate mouldings and a star-studded history. Every famous person in Liverpool seemed to have used it as their local at one time or another; and it gave me a thrill to imagine I might be sitting in the same seat George Harrison once sat in.

We all hung around in the college snack bar until it was nearly six. Joss had turned up by this time, grumbling because the shop had told her she would have to wait a few days while they ordered the new part for her instrument. When we got to the Phil, it was to find that Mel had beaten us to it and had already lined up drinks for us.

'White wine all right, girls?' he enquired cheerfully. I saw Joss grit her teeth – her usual drink was lager – but she didn't say anything.

As soon as we were all settled round a table, he began to discuss the arrangements for our festival appearance.

'I've got you a Transit van and a couple of roadies, Denis and Tom. They're old hands – they've been with various bands for years. Status Quo, Queen – you name it. Denis'll do your mixing, too. He's the electronics expert.'

'What do we need a van for? We've still got my cousin's,' Pip pointed out.

'What – that old thing? I wouldn't like to trust it getting you any further than Speke!' he scoffed, and Pip glared at him.

'Look, you girls shouldn't have to do your own driving, it's not right for your image and it's not fair on you. You need all your energy for your show and how can you do a good gig if you're exhausted from map-reading, tyre-changing and having your bones rattled for two hundred miles? You're on at eleven-thirty, so I think it would be best if you drove down the night before and we got you put up at a motel.'

'Who's going to pay for that?' Ireka asked suspiciously.

'Katzco – who else?' said Mel, giving the name of his

management company.

'You need a tax loss, then, do you?' Joss shot quickly.

Mel gave a quick grin. 'Let's just call it an investment of faith. If things work out as I think they will for you girls, then my initial loss should be repaid many times over. So don't you worry your pretty heads about that.' He reached out and tweaked Ireka's braids as he spoke, and she backed off, startled.

'What we desperately need now is a record,' Mel announced, and we all sat up sharply. 'It would be great if you could announce to all those thousands of people at the festival that you had a single due out. I might be able to get it played on some local radio station down there. Anything coming from Merseyside is news at the moment. I don't suppose you fancy changing your name to Francesca Goes to Holyhead? No? Never mind, that *was* a joke,' he added, catching Joss's eye. But it was okay – she was grinning.

We spent the next hour suggesting this song and that, cover versions of golden oldies, slightly altered versions of songs we did already, but nothing seemed to be right.

'It's no use releasing an anti-men song because you're instantly alienating half your potential record buyers,' Mel said sagely. 'Keep all that in the act, for sure, but for your single you need something with more general appeal to everyone. Haven't you got *anything*? I'd like it to be a song of yours, because that way you'll keep the songwriting royalties and earn more.'

I don't know what made me say it, but I suddenly blurted out, 'I've got something which might be okay.

The others haven't heard it yet, but . . .'

Three pairs of hotly accusing eyes gazed at me. 'Do you mean to say you've got some good stuff and been keeping it to yourself?' Pip snapped.

'I don't know if it's good or not, that's why I haven't brought it along to rehearsal. Anyway, I haven't got a tune for it yet,' I explained defensively.

After that, the others badgered me non-stop. But how could I show them *Chapters*? It was far too personal. Maybe I'd be able to write something else quickly, and kid them that that was the song I'd meant.

But inspiration didn't come, and the next night I went along to Joss's with the lyrics thrust reluctantly into my guitar case.

'Shona, I'm ashamed of you – it's a *love* song,' said Pip in disgust.

'I think it's great,' Ireka said loyally. 'I've felt all those things myself.'

'I think it's good . . . *really* good.' Joss spoke quietly, and I couldn't believe I'd heard her properly. *She* liked it? But, come to think of it, I reminded myself, Joss had changed a bit lately. She wasn't quite as stridently anti-men as she used to be. In fact, she'd become somewhat reserved, taking more of a back seat in the group's organization and letting the rest of us have more of a say. All I could think of was that perhaps Pip had had a row with her and put her in her place.

'What do you think Mel will say?' I ventured.

'It's not worth showing him a set of song lyrics, he hasn't any imagination. No, we'll have to get a tune written first,' Ireka insisted. I knew she'd disliked Mel ever since he'd grabbed her hair in the pub. 'I'm not going to let him treat me like a little girl,' she'd insisted afterwards, feeling most insulted.

'Well, I hereby hand my masterpiece over to you,' I declared ceremoniously, and gave Joss the sheet of paper. Then we launched ourselves into a couple of hours of hard practising.

Of course, I had to confess to my parents that I was going to disappear over the Easter weekend, and so I got the whole gamut of complaints and moans: 'You'll fail your exams if you mess around with this group'; 'You'll get in with the wrong sort of people. We don't want a daughter of ours on drink and drugs', etc., etc. Fortunately, Kate was with me as I tried to explain and loyally stood up for me, telling them it wasn't that sort of band, and that we were all sensible people.

Then, on Sunday night, Kate and I assembled at Joss's place, to await our van and the roadies! Mel had some friends in Milton Keynes who'd offered to put us all up for the night, so long as we didn't mind sleeping on the floor. Naturally, I had to assure my parents that Kate and I would have a bedroom to ourselves – and would lock the door firmly! We had sleeping bags at home, so I borrowed two and, at 6 p.m., off we set.

Chapter Thirteen

'Don't you think you ought to save your voice, Shona?' Ireka whispered worriedly, as we all bowled down the M6 singing at the tops of our voices.

'I wish Tom would save his fingers,' I muttered back. Having given up on Pip, who had threatened to brain him with her bass, he was now having a go at me and his arm kept creeping along the back of the seat and ruffling my hair in the most annoying manner.

Denis was driving, so at least Ireka was safe for now – though we were dreading what might happen once we got to Mel's friends' place.

They turned out to be nice, but pretty weird. Paul was about Mel's age – it turned out they'd been to school together – but his wife, Krystina, looked more like his mother. She was not only years older than he was, but larger in every respect, including her hearty nature, and she greeted us in rapturous heavily accented English, and insisted on treating all seven of us to a monumental fry-up, washed down with cans of lager.

Their house was built on a hillside, sort of split level, and everything seemed to be up and down steps, even the bathroom. Denis and Tom were dragged off by Paul to his club, where they could get a drink after pub-closing time. Krystina explained the sleeping arrangements, which were that the two boys would take the front room, and we girls could divide ourselves between the spare bedroom and the downstairs back room.

We drew lots for the bedroom, and Kate and I won. Next morning, we heard that the others had had a wretched time, with Denis and Tom trying to get into their room even though they'd barricaded it with furniture and wedged a chair beneath the handle. But Kate and I had had an almost equally bad time being kept awake by the loo flushing at regular and frequent intervals, as the three guys worked their way through vast amounts of home-brewed beer.

However, we had worse things to worry about in the morning than tiredness — a twitch of the curtains revealed that the weather had changed unexpectedly overnight, and it was tipping down with rain.

'Oh, *no* — I can't believe it!' I groaned.

'Do you think they'll call it off?' Ireka wondered.

After a consultation, we decided to ring Mel, who assured us that the show was on, come rain or shine. And so we set off dispiritedly for the soggy festival site.

Instead of the cheering crowds we'd hoped to play to, there were little clusters of people in dripping anoraks, sheltering beneath umbrellas, or even remaining in their tents for protection.

Our appearance elicited a thin spatter of applause, and we felt so despondent that we couldn't be bothered to try and get our audience going; we just plodded through six numbers as quickly as possible, and left the (fortunately covered) stage to a deafening silence.

'Well, what else could we do?' challenged Joss. 'The thing was a literal wash-out.'

'We were lucky we weren't electrocuted, with all

that water around,' I observed.

'Come on, let's get back, I've got a back-stage pass for Princess at the Apollo tonight,' Denis grunted, and he and Tom began loading up our gear.

'Oh Kate, I'm so sorry I had to drag you all the way down here for this,' I apologized, as we got in the back of the vehicle along with Pip and Tom. Ireka always had to travel in the front, otherwise she got sick. 'I honestly don't know if it's worth carrying on, you know. This hasn't done us any good whatsoever . . .'

Pip sighed. 'Just put it down to experience. Though I must admit a few more experiences like this and I'll be thinking of selling a bass guitar!'

'I know someone who can sell you a better one than that thing you've got,' Tom offered.

'There's nothing wrong with my guitar – and will you *stop* sticking your leg against mine!' Pip spat.

It was gloom and arguments all the way home, and we finally parted company in the middle of town with no further plans for rehearsals until after the holidays, which was quite a relief. By Thursday, the weather had picked up again, so we got our day in Wales. Mum drove us out there and the three of us exclaimed in delight over the fields full of lambs. We ate sandwiches while sitting perched on rocks high above a valley, with only the bleating of sheep and the crying of curlews for company. It was completely refreshing, and only once or twice did I find myself wishing Rob was with us; I instantly banished thoughts of him by chattering brightly and making Mum laugh with an impression of Gina Smith giving us shorthand dictation.

Darryl popped over a couple of times while Kate was

with us, and we went out in a threesome. He was a nice guy, even though he liked to wear red and orange, which clashed horribly with his ginger hair. I told Kate that the coast was clear if she fancied him, but she said she didn't, and that no-one could ever replace Dave. I knew exactly how she felt.

Kate had decided to spend half the Easter vacation with me, and half with her own parents. I felt at a bit of a loose end after she'd gone, but I'd brought some lecture notes and books with me and got down to some long overdue studying. After all, it wasn't very long to the end-of-year exams, and I wanted to make sure I passed, even if my marks weren't very high.

One afternoon Darryl came round to show off his new car, a bright green French thing which really did look like a frog! We drove to one of the local beauty spots, up on a hill overlooking an island on the River Dee which had a bird sanctuary on it.

It was a pity I didn't feel anything for Darryl, I mused as we strolled along, linking arms like the old friends we were. There was no tingle where any bits of me touched him; if he had been Rob, my arm would have felt on fire.

'What are you planning to do with yourself?' I asked, knowing he'd been out of work since he left school the previous summer.

'I might work as a lifeguard for a bit –' (Darryl was a great swimmer and had loads of certificates) '– but what I was really wondering – if *you* don't mind, that is – was if I could work with your group. You know, driving, or being your roadie, or something. You know how mad on the music scene I am . . .'

I threw back my head and laughed. 'Oh, Darryl,' I gasped through my merriment, 'you won't get any money doing that. We only just about cover our expenses ourselves! Anyway, we're stuck with these awful blokes –' and I told him about Denis and Tom.

'I don't care about the money,' he replied ardently. 'Just promise you'll let me know if anything comes up.'

I promised, though I very much doubted if there'd ever be anything for him, and I'd hate letting him down . . .

Pip rang up the evening I got back to my digs. 'Thank goodness!' she exclaimed. 'I've been going mad trying to find out where your parents lived, so that I could ring you. Can you come round to Joss's?'

'But I've only just got back – I haven't even unpacked,' I wailed.

'Then we'll come round to you,' she arranged briskly, and replaced the receiver before I could object.

Forty minutes later, they were filing into my untidy room.

'Well, it's our biggest break yet!' Joss bubbled. I'd never seen her looking so excited. 'Mel's got us a tour – imagine that!'

'A tour of what? Siberia? Cruise missile bases?' I joked.

'Birmingham, Brighton, er . . . St Austell, wherever that may be –'

'Cornwall,' I informed her. 'Where else?'

'Portsmouth and – guess what? – London! The Marquee Club – isn't that incredible?'

It was pandemonium for the next five minutes, while

we all yelled and babbled. 'Does Ireka know yet?' I enquired.

'Yes. We saw her yesterday. Oh, and there's something else. We've got a melody for your song. Here it is – get practising.' Joss tossed a cassette onto my bed.

As soon as they'd gone, I fed it into the tape player. The voice and the piano playing which filled the room were Joss's, her sweet, light contralto doing little with the words. But the melody was incredible. I felt tears welling up in my eyes and I sank down onto the rug, hugging my knees to me. It was nostalgic, haunting, bitter, perfect. I couldn't have composed it in a month of Sundays. To think that Joss had written this – she must have been truly inspired. She immediately went up about nine million rungs in my estimation.

And there was something else too, which I felt in my bones and which set all the hairs on my arms and the back of my neck rising. It seemed immodest, to feel like this about my own song – well, *half*-song – but I felt utterly positive, absolutely solidly sure, that it could be a hit . . .

Chapter Fourteen

Mel thought so too. 'We'll try it out on the tour and see how it goes down with the audiences,' he said guardedly. 'Any other new songs you've got, let's have 'em. Might as well use this tour as a testing ground to see which of your stuff is the most popular. Now, I want to say a few things about presentation. At the moment, you're far too rigid, the lot of you – even you, Shona. I'd like to see you and Pip doing a kind of double-act – you must have seen guitarists walking up to each other on stage and dancing together, playing little musical phrases and chords and echoing each other. Just watch all the TV pop shows put out over the next week or so, study the videos, you'll soon see what I mean.

'And Joss, I'd like to see you leave the synthesizers and be the front man – er, person – for one of the numbers. Stand next to Shona, share her mike for the harmonies, get the audience going. You know how to do it!'

Mel continued with his pep talk and I listened excitedly. This tour wasn't *just* us, of course; I mean, who'd want to come if we were top of the bill? No-one outside Liverpool (and very few inside) had ever heard of us. No, we were the warm-up act to Male Order, a bunch of very pretty boys who had quite a fan following. It would be interesting to see how *we* went down with their largely female audience, I thought. And it was exciting to think that there would be a proper advertising campaign, with posters, and ads in the music papers, bearing our name: *Male Order, support band Zero*. Mel said he was trying to get us some press and local radio interviews, too. I was burning with anticipation. Now, for the first time ever, I could actually visualize success just around the corner. Study and classes receded into a kind of never-never land.

The reason why we had landed this tour was because the original support band had recently split up and the tour organizers had had to find a last-minute replacement, which wasn't easy as most bands had got themselves bookings. Fortunately, someone had thought of asking Mel who he had on his books – and so here we were, all set to go with just two weeks in which to practise like mad!

'What are we going to do about college?' Ireka asked worriedly, as we sat around at Joss's that evening. 'We can't just not turn up for a whole week. One of us might get away with it, but not all four.'

'Have faith, sister!' intoned Pip, tossing her lank locks. 'Who needs a diploma in business studies, or a certificate of a hundred words per minute shorthand, if they've got a single at number one?'

'I wish he'd listened to us about Denis and Tom,' I grumbled. 'And another thing . . . Mel had a grope at me as we left the office. You mightn't have seen it, but I felt it.'

'The rat,' hissed Joss. 'Why don't you pinch *his* bum next time you see him, and give him a taste of his own medicine? That's what we should all do to men who try it on.'

'The trouble is, they'd probably like it,' Ireka observed, with a mock sigh.

'I do want to say thanks again for what you did with my song,' I told Joss, from the bottom of my heart.

She went a bit pink. 'Well, I had a little help,' she demurred.

'Well, thanks to everyone who helped!' I added.

Two hours of solid practice later, with Maggie from

downstairs rocking baby Simon to the rhythms, I dragged myself home – and found a froglike car parked under the street lamp outside my house.

Darryl leapt out as soon as he saw me. 'Just called by on the off-chance, seeing as I was in town,' he greeted me, then added: 'Well, been here about an hour, actually. I thought you must be out with some fella!'

For some reason, his careless remark really annoyed me, but I still felt obliged to ask him in for a coffee, which was okay as there was no landlady on the premises – she only turned up once a week to collect the rent.

The first thing he wanted to know about was the roadie business, and he looked most disappointed when I told him we were still saddled with Denis and Tom – and he was positively green with envy when he heard about the tour.

'Listen, if I can get you a ticket for our London gig, will you come?' I invited, and the eager expression on his face made the offer worth while.

After a pretty heavy smooching session, which I didn't really enjoy, I managed to get rid of him. It was about one o'clock in the morning, so heaven only knew what time he'd get home.

'I hope I'll see you before the London gig,' he said hopefully.

'I don't know. We'll be rehearsing most nights,' I pointed out, but he ended up persuading me to invite him to a rehearsal. I was dreading what Joss's and Pip's reaction would be!

I got round it by suggesting to the others that we gave a kind of dress rehearsal to a group of friends a few days before the tour. Mel was all in favour and hired a church hall for the occasion. Kate came, Darryl, the inevitable Keith Randall who made a nuisance of himself by bothering Kate all evening, Mike, and a whole crowd of people from the poly – but there was no sign of Rob. I spent the first three numbers scanning the hall for him, then gave up. It was probably better this way, I reminded myself, because he might have turned up with that girl and I wouldn't have been able to stand it.

Mel upset the lot of us by insisting that, for the tour, we wore something other than our usual baggy flying suits.

'This is your chance to impress people – you've got to look different,' he said, in his drawling voice. 'Come to my office at one-thirty tomorrow. I've got a friend who's a designer and she'll fix you up.'

'It could have been worse,' I said afterwards. 'He could have wanted us to wear dresses like Dolly Parton.'

'If I didn't think he was doing a good job, I'd burn this in front of his eyes,' thundered Joss, holding at arm's length the black leotard with the silver Z zig-zagging from elbow to hip. Skin-tight black stretch satin jeans, silver legwarmers and ankle boots completed the outfit. I thought it was quite nice myself and Ireka really loved it.

We found we weren't to be staying in the same hotels as Male Order during the tour. We didn't quite merit Holiday Inns yet, apparently.

'CBS Records are quite interested in hearing you,' Mel told us as a morale-booster, the day before we were due to leave. 'In fact, there should be several talent scouts from various companies dropping in, so play your hearts out, girls.' He winked, and I was sure it was a lecherous one. He was joining us halfway through the tour, and would be with us in Portsmouth and London, and I felt a nasty shudder at the thought of him trying to get off with me. Funny how a guy can seem quite nice at first, then pretty soon show his true colours as a creep!

In the days leading up to the tour, we went to the very minimum of lectures, praying that our absence wouldn't be noted. Then, suddenly, as if time had accelerated and covered about five days in one, we were speeding down the motorway towards Birmingham.

'Denis, will you keep your eyes on the road and your hands to yourself!' Pip shrieked, for about the fifth time. I was having enough trouble in the back of the big van, trying to stop Tom's arm from snaking round my neck, and his hand from straying across my boobs. He really was loathsome.

'Cut it out, fellas,' drawled Joss, in a passable imitation of Mel.

I heaved a deep sigh. Were we really going to have to put up with this for five days?

The furniture in our cheap hotel in a Birmingham back street seemed to be made out of cardboard; a leg on one of the chairs buckled the minute I sat down on it.

'The whole hotel's a cardboard cut-out,' chortled Joss. 'Maybe the whole of *Birmingham* is!'

But our audience that night certainly wasn't. They

were slow to respond at first, and we had to put up with calls of, 'Male *Order*, Male *Order*,' between our first couple of numbers. But then they seemed to get into the music, and our lines poking fun at blokes started going down very well with all the girls. At the end, they all cheered and I walked off the stage feeling really high, as if we'd achieved something splendid. It was the first time we'd played to so many people and when I first saw the crowd, I nearly passed out. It looked like millions, though I was assured there were only about a thousand.

Our faithful roadies ferried us back to our hotel, then disappeared.

'Thank God for that,' we all chorused – but we spoke too soon, for into the foyer clanked Denis and Tom with two bulging carrier bags full of cans and bottles.

'Party time, girls,' announced Tom with a broad grin.

'Get lost,' snarled Pip.

'Oh, come on, first night of the tour and all that. Just a little sociable drink,' Den pleaded, and we ended up having to give in, and all crowding into the tiny room I was sharing with Ireka. It was three in the morning before we got rid of the guys, and that was only after a complaint from the occupant of the next bedroom.

We were up again at eight, absolutely exhausted, and after a nauseatingly greasy plateful of egg, bacon and a sausage, we hit the road. Our spirits rose as we neared Brighton, though. The sun was out and when we caught sight of the vivid blue sea, we all cheered.

'Who's for a dip?' I yelled.

'We haven't brought our cossies,' Ireka wailed.

'I don't mind skinny-dipping,' leered Denis, and we all groaned.

We compromised by paddling instead, then we went off to the concert hall for a sound-check. Male Order were there ahead of us, and a pretty stand-offish lot they were, too. It was the first time we'd seen them to speak to.

'Watch out, boys, here comes Women's Lib,' yelled a spotty guy with masses of peroxided hair. He was the drummer, and I was quite amused to note that in the flesh, close up, these pin-up boys weren't nearly as perfect as they looked on their posters.

'You're just jealous because Birmingham liked us better than you,' Pip screeched. 'They're all a load of poofs, anyway,' she added in an undertone. 'I read it in a music paper.' And we all giggled.

The upshot was that our precious headlining act messed around for so long that we had no time for a sound-check. We felt sure they'd done it deliberately.

We always found we couldn't eat before a show as we were far too keyed-up; so now we went for a walk along the sea front, which wasn't far from our hotel, then back to the concert hall. It didn't take long to discover that the audience was vastly different to the appreciative Birmingham crowd. Lukewarm applause and indifferent expressions greeted even our most frenzied efforts to put some life into the proceedings, and afterwards Tom and Denis disappeared on a pub crawl, leaving us to hold a gloomy post mortem.

'I'm glad Mel wasn't here,' I said. 'He'd probably have sacked us. They didn't even like *Chapters*.'

'They've got no taste,' Joss said loyally. To unwind, we watched telly for a bit, then all went to bed.

It was a long drive to Cornwall next day. On arrival, we didn't even have time to check in at our hotel, but had to go straight to the concert hall. About twenty minutes before we were due to go on, I paid a visit to the loo and found Joss sagging against the wall.

'Are you all right?' I asked, concerned.

'No,' she grunted – then rushed into one of the cubicles and locked the door. I could hear her being sick.

I raced off to get Pip, and we waited anxiously for Joss to re-emerge. When she did, her face was grey and she was clutching her stomach.

'It's my own fault,' she gasped. 'Those shellfish we got from the stall –'

'We're all okay,' I pointed out.

'I should have known better,' she whispered weakly. 'I was allergic to them as a kid, but I thought I'd be all right by now.'

'Is there anything we can do?' I said, then glanced at my watch. 'Oh God, we're nearly due on. What are we going to do?'

Joss's answer was to dash into the loo again. I stared agonizedly at Pip. 'We can't manage without her – we'll have to cancel it.'

'We *can't*,' she replied, her face distorted with worry. She raked a hand through her hair. 'Couldn't you dash out to a chemist's and get some pills?'

'No time – and anyway, I don't know where the nearest shops are,' I pointed out.

Just then Ireka burst in. 'What's going on?' she

shouted. 'The promoter's going crazy. They're ready to announce us!'

'Joss is ill,' I said dully.

'Well, we'll have to manage without her somehow,' Ireka snapped. I knew she wasn't really cross, just tense as hell like the rest of us.

Then Joss staggered out again. 'I'll – I'll be all right,' she grunted. 'Just get me a glass of water.'

She was too weak to change into her costume. We were announced, and she slunk behind her bank of keyboards — her original small system had been augmented, thanks to Mel — and, with rather less enthusiasm than usual, we limped into our first number.

Just how Joss got through the next half hour, I shall never know, but she did. When we were back in our dressing-room and she was lying full length along a bench with a wet flannel across her forehead, a girl came in with a portable tape recorder. She introduced herself as Carol Hughes, a reporter from a local paper, and as soon as she learned of Joss's predicament, she was overjoyed.

'What a great story!' she crowed. 'That's what I call guts!'

'*Lack* of guts, you mean,' Joss commented weakly. 'I think I've lost most of them!'

The reporter asked us all about Zero, and then enquired if we had a record in the pipeline. We all glanced frantically at each other, then Ireka said confidently, 'It's not quite signed, sealed and delivered yet, but our first disc will probably be the song we ended with, *Chapters*. Shona wrote it.'

'Nice song,' the girl said. 'Good luck to all of you. I

hope to see Zero at the top of the hit parade.'

'Fat chance,' scoffed Pip after she'd gone. We dragged poor Joss into the van and drove gingerly to our hotel, where the girl at the reception desk managed to find something to help settle her stomach.

The next morning, I struggled up from dreamland to reality, spurred by the ringing of the telephone. It was Mel, to say he'd meet us in Portsmouth at three. 'Good work, girlies,' he said breezily. 'Nice piece – very nice.'

'What are you talking about?' I managed to utter, with Ireka tugging at my arm, demanding to know what was being said.

Imagine my amazement when I discovered that Carol Hughes, the girl who'd interviewed us, had managed to sell her story to one of the national daily papers! Not only that, but they'd also got hold of a photograph of us that some local photographer had taken at the concert.

I was about to leap up, rush out and buy a copy when Ireka reminded me: 'What are roadies for?' and so I rang their room number and ordered them to get us two copies each. I wanted to keep one and send the other to Mum and Dad, and I felt sure the others would want to do something similar.

Joss seemed much better, for which we were all mightily relieved. We didn't want anything to happen to mar our final and most important gig, the one in London . . .

Denis came back with the papers, and we all sat over breakfast, giggling about the report.

'Look – they've spelt my name wrong,' complained Ireka. '*Eureka*, indeed!'

99

'You're just a blob in the background,' I said commiseratingly to Joss.

'Just as well. It's a wonder I appeared at all – I felt like a ghost!'

It was only a short paragraph, about ten lines, but I felt so proud. They'd even mentioned the title of our single . . .

'What's this?' Mel thundered, when we strolled into the foyer of our Portsmouth hotel and he came leaping up to meet us. 'It didn't hit me at first, but we're in trouble. Who told them about the record?'

'I'm afraid it was me,' Ireka confessed.

'Well, I'm going to look a bloody fool if I can't get anyone to release it, aren't I?' Mel snapped.

'You'd just better get us a record deal then, hadn't you?' Joss answered silkily, as he glared at her.

'I was going to do so, anyway. I told you there were going to be a few important people at the London show tomorrow. So it's up to you now, you'd better surpass yourselves.'

'Don't we always?' Joss replied cheekily, and Mel clicked his tongue petulantly. He was wearing jeans and shoes of such a dazzling whiteness that I almost held my breath for fear of anything, a speck of dust, a drip from somebody's drink, landing on them.

'Oh hell, my costume's still damp,' I grumbled as I went to put it on before our show that night. It had smelt so horribly stale and sweaty after being worn for three whole performances that I'd rinsed it out in the washbasin in our room and then hung it over the radiator; I'd felt sure it was dry when I'd stuck it in my bag that morning.

That night, we were great – even Male Order buried the hatchet, greeting us afterwards with encouraging words of praise. I ended up having a really interesting conversation with their guitarist about the different sounds made by different makes of guitar. It made me realize how much I'd still got to learn.

We went to bed that night with the sounds of cheers and cries of *'Encore'* ringing in our ears. The next morning I woke up with an absolutely excruciating sore throat . . .

Chapter Fifteen

'I'll get you to a doctor as soon as we get to London. In the meantime, keep absolutely quiet, don't say a word to anyone. Just rest those vocal cords,' Mel ordered.

I had to wait until my cup of tea went tepid before I could drink it, and it even hurt to swallow soft bread and butter. 'It must be tonsillitis,' I whispered huskily.

'Shut up!' snapped Mel, looking most anxious. 'We've got to get you better for tonight, so much depends on it.'

The others all looked at me sympathetically. 'Just do what Mel says, Shona,' Ireka said soothingly. 'I'm sure a doctor will be able to give you some pain-killers or something.'

'I bloody well hope so,' I mouthed.

All the way to London, I lamented my bad luck. Why couldn't it have happened tomorrow? I thought. By then, I'd be safely home and even if I went down with appendicitis, it wouldn't matter. Well . . . it would, really — I certainly didn't *want* to get appendicitis!

Mel had come down in his own car, and Denis had opted to travel with him, to make a bit of extra room in the van. Without another guy to egg him on, Tom was much quieter. We arrived at the outskirts of London and I was amazed at how long it took to reach the centre; we seemed to travel for miles, passing more and more houses, rows of shops and sets of traffic lights.

We managed to lose Mel and Denis twice, but each time they waited somewhere for us to catch up, and finally we drew up behind them at a hotel in what looked like an entire street of similar establishments.

'Sorry it's not the Hilton,' Mel apologized. 'I'll go and ring this doctor I know and see if he can fit you in. He's a Harley Street guy and has a lot of showbiz people on his books. I — er — I'm afraid this'll have to come out of your wages, girls. The old budget won't stretch to private medicine.'

'But this is an emergency!' Joss shouted, oblivious to the looks we were getting from passers-by.

'Why can't I see a National Health doctor?' I croaked.

'Not a word from you,' Mel threatened. 'And you know the answer: it's because you have to arrange to be ill days in advance. You can't just walk into a surgery without an appointment, unless you're practically dying, and I don't think they'd consider a rock concert a life-or-death affair!'

He went off to telephone, then came back, took my arm and led me to his car, telling the others to get their stuff up to their rooms and wait.

My first thought on seeing Dr Blake, after being smiled and simpered at by his white-coated receptionist, was that I must have walked into a television soap opera. He was, quite simply, gorgeous, in his late thirties, maybe, very dark and distinguished, his hair slightly greying at the temples to give him the perfect look of kindly authority.

'And what have we here? A songbird who's lost her warble?' he joked and I had to try hard not to laugh.

I opened my mouth wide as directed and my heart beat wildly as he stepped close to me and peered down my throat with the aid of a flashlight.

'Hmm, a trifle inflamed. Been training as a fire-eater in case you don't make Number One? I'd better prescribe antibiotics and you just rest that voice, young lady. You could do it serious damage by straining it.'

'But she's got to sing tonight,' Mel pointed out worriedly.

'I wouldn't advise it,' the doctor replied sternly. 'Not unless she's got the Albert Hall sold out.'

'Please . . .' I said hoarsely.

'You must be aware of the risk you're taking. It's your own decision, and it's against my medical advice,' the doctor warned, shaking his handsome head. 'All right, then.' He scribbled something on a sheet of paper and tore it off his pad. I looked at it. It was nothing like an ordinary prescription. It was just a scribble on a piece of paper, with his signature and a rubber stamp giving the address of the surgery. 'Good luck, I hope it goes well,' he said, and gave me a sudden, breathtaking smile.

Mel ordered me to wait outside for him while he sorted out the bill, after which we drove to the nearest chemist.

The doctor's instructions were to start taking the antibiotics immediately, and to use the throat spray once now and then use it again just before going on stage. So I gave my tonsils a good blasting and a few minutes later, I got the sensation one gets when the dentist has administered a numbing injection. The back of my throat felt freezing cold and sort of dead and I felt as if I were going to choke, but I gradually got used to the feeling.

'Dr Blake said you mustn't even try to sing until tonight. And you must eat only soft things today, like scrambled egg, or soup,' Mel ordered. I grimaced. The others had just announced their intention of going for a Wendyburger, and I'd have given anything to join them. Having been deprived of breakfast, my stomach was complaining like mad. The rumbles would probably be audible through the microphone tonight, I thought glumly.

'Cheer up,' Joss said sympathetically. 'We'll all sing louder to make up for you.'

That day really dragged. I didn't bother to go to the sound-check – Ireka, who had the next loudest voice to mine, promised to test my microphones for me.

At seven-thirty, we strolled into the Marquee and at first I thought we must have come to the wrong place. After the modern halls we'd been playing in, this place was tiny. It was cramped and dingy and I didn't see how it could hold even a hundred people without them getting squashed to death. But I'd heard of the club, and all the amazing people who'd played there, including the Rolling Stones, the Police and just about every famous rock musician you could think of, and I hoped some of the magic would rub off on us.

'Oh God, I hope I'll be all right. I don't want to let you lot down,' I said anxiously in the dressing-room. I'd tried out a few experimental la-la's and they sounded all right, but I didn't know how my voice was going to stand up to one song after another.

The rest of the group made encouraging noises, and then we were on.

I'd been advised to make the introduction as brief as possible and not to chat between numbers. Instead, Joss took over this chore. Halfway through our first song, I was aware that the others were sounding superb, especially Ireka, who was really beating her drum kit to death. I smiled. I knew they were all trying harder than usual, to give me courage and strength.

By the third song, I was singing as loudly as usual, yet I was aware I didn't have my normal tone and couldn't force my vocal cords to produce all the effects they were usually capable of. Then – disaster – I cracked on a top note and could have died of embarrassment – and it was at that moment that I saw him . . . *Rob*! He was leaning against the side of the archway that led into the back bar. He had a pint glass in his hand and raised it to me and grinned.

It was as if a good witch had waved a wand and cast a magic spell over me. I felt a surge of energy and I relaxed and opened my throat, instead of letting fear and worry cramp it up. My eyes swept the room and I spotted other people I knew. Kate was there, and Keith Randall, of all people, and Dave Simmonds – heavens, that was going to upset Kate! Then I saw Darryl and he waved to me. But I only had eyes for Rob . . .

I think you know when you're really giving everything you've got. I hurled myself into each number, remembering what Mel had said about moving and getting into it. I plucked notes out of my guitar that I'd never tried before, and played chords I didn't know I knew, and Joss and Pip responded, filling in with new runs and melodies.

Then it was time for our last number, *Chapters;* suddenly, I wished I were anywhere else in the universe but here. What if Rob should guess that I'd written the song about him and me? Then I reasoned with myself; why should he? It could be about someone I'd known before him, or even pure imagination. Anyway, why should he bother his head about it? His girlfriend was probably around somewhere, buried in the gyrating crowd.

So I sang it – and the applause and cheers erupted even before the last note had died away. We played an encore – our version of *Dancing in The Dark* by Bruce Springsteen. We could have done another, and another, but the club manager was signalling that our time was up and they had to start the interval now.

I was shaking as I sank onto a chair in the dressing-room. Sweat was pouring off me and taking my costume off was like peeling off a wet swimsuit.

'Let's go and mingle with the others and have a

drink,' Pip suggested, so we left Denis and Tom with the task of taking our stuff back to the van which was parked some distance away owing to the traffic regulations in Wardour Street and came out into the bar nearest the entrance.

I saw Mel deep in conversation with two guys. 'He should be buying the drinks,' Joss grumbled, 'after what we put into tonight's performance. We worked our whatsits off for him and he hasn't even come over to thank us.'

But our friends did. Darryl insisted on buying a round for everyone. I was hoping he wouldn't hang around me, just in case there was any chance of my being with Rob, but he plainly had ideas of his own and proceeded to manoeuvre Ireka into a corner. Pip noticed and winked at me.

Kate forced her way through the crowd and came over to me. 'You and Joss are in dead trouble,' she said concernedly. I nudged Joss to make sure she was listening. 'Gina went mad when you didn't turn up all week, and none of us could think of any excuses that could cover two people for a whole week. She's set us a really important test for Monday and says that anyone who doesn't pass won't be allowed to enter for their finals. It may just be an empty threat, but you never know with her. I thought I ought to warn you.'

I groaned. Tests . . . at an exciting time like this? The last thing I wanted to think about was college. Now I'd have to work like stink all weekend, when I'd been looking forward to relaxing and enjoying myself – and perhaps celebrating something, too, if Mel had managed to finalize any kind of deal for us. He was still talking to those guys in the corner of the bar.

Kate started rhapsodizing about how marvellous we were and I started telling her about my throat, but my attention began to wander as I caught myself looking for Rob. Where was he? Didn't he even care enough to want to congratulate us? Or was it that he still felt so sore about not being part of Zero any more?

Keith Randall came up and began to monopolize the conversation, telling Kate and Pip some joke he'd just heard. I muttered an excuse and began to thread my way through the crowd, but it was difficult because total strangers kept wanting to talk to me about Zero and where we were going to be playing next. I should have been thrilled, but all I could think of was how I was going to feel when I saw Rob with his arm round that girl.

But he wasn't in the back bar or in the main room and, bewildered, I retraced my footsteps.

'Shona!' I whirled round. It was Rob and, miracle of miracles, he was alone. He beckoned to me and I saw he was looking somewhat agitated. As soon as I drew level with him he caught my elbow and pulled me round the corner.

'Shona, just how deep in are you with this Mel Katz? Have you signed anything?'

'Yes, of course we have. Why?' I asked. I'd never seen Rob looking so stern.

'Has he got you a record deal yet?'

'I jolly well hope so,' I replied tartly. What business was it of his?

'Well, don't let him make you sign anything else

until you've taken the contract to a specialist lawyer. I think the man's a crook.'

'You what?' I answered incredulously. 'What right have you to say that? Are you sure you're not just jealous, and trying to stir up trouble and ruin things?'

'My God, Shona, just what sort of a person do you think I am? Do you really think so little of me?' Rob said huskily.

With all the cigarette smoke in the air, my throat was beginning to hurt again. However it was too soon to use the throat spray again and anyway, I'd left it in the dressing-room. So I replied to his question with a confused shake of the head.

'Do you honestly think I'd have slaved for days to write that melody for Joss's song if I didn't care about Zero?'

His words hit my ears like a thunderclap. '*You* wrote that melody?' I squeaked, my mind reeling under the double impact of what he'd just said. 'But . . . I thought Joss . . . Anyway, it's not her song, it's mine. I don't know what you're talking about.' I put my hand to my forehead, feeling slightly faint.

Then I felt Rob's hand taking by elbow. 'Let's get out of here, find somewhere quieter,' he suggested, and I nodded eagerly.

He said something to one of the guys behind the bar, and the next minute someone had opened a door and I found myself in a small, dark alleyway. Rob and I walked side by side in silence until we reached the street, where there was a pub on the corner. He ushered me into the bar, which wasn't exactly empty, but it was a lot quieter than the packed-out club.

'What would you like?' he asked.

I grimaced. 'Anything that's good for sore throats.'

'Rum and blackcurrant, that's the stuff. I'll see if they can give you a hot one.' He parked me at a table and came back with the drinks a few minutes later. 'Cheers,' he said, raising his pint of bitter. 'Now I'll tell you something I heard this evening, and if this won't make you distrust that manager of yours, nothing will . . .'

Chapter Sixteen

'And who was this man Mel was talking to?' My throat was feeling a bit better now; the rum and blackcurrant – lukewarm, the best the barman could manage – was obviously doing the trick.

'I don't know for sure, but from the gist of the conversation I gathered his name was Eddie and he was from a record company, because they were discussing percentages various people would get from record sales and – I'm sorry to have to say this, Shona, but they really think they're dealing with a load of starry-eyed, star-struck innocents. I mean, they were actually laughing about how much money they were hoping to make out of you.'

Rob elaborated on what he'd overheard, and I felt

utterly sick. If he was right, then Zero was about to be taken for a ride. *If* Rob was right. There were an awful lot of things I didn't quite understand, which needed clearing up – like, for instance, how Rob just happened to know who Mel was, when he had never met him. I asked him.

'Oh dear, I knew I'd have to tell you sooner or later. Look, can I get us another drink first?' he begged, and I nodded. As I watched him walk over to the bar, threading his way between the tables, I couldn't help but admire his back view, his well-cut hair, his strong shoulders, his lovely neat bottom and his legs which were well-shaped without being too lumpy and muscley. Why did I have to find him so attractive? I asked myself despairingly. I'd had plenty of time to get over him. Why hadn't I gone off him in all this time, especially as I knew the situation was useless and pointless? *He's got a girlfriend,* I reminded myself, gritting my teeth as he walked towards me with a heart-melting smile.

'Right . . . confession time. Joss brought me a certain set of songwords, saying she'd written them. Normally, I wouldn't have believed her, but as I knew what was going on –'

He stopped and glanced speculatively at me. 'You don't know? Oh, I'd better keep my big mouth shut then,' he said, infuriatingly. 'Anyway, she said she wanted it to be a secret between her and me about me writing the tune, because she didn't know how the others would feel about my involvement. But she made an appointment for me to go and see Mel, to talk about publishing rights, and it was she who invited me to come tonight, so that I could hear the finished product . . .'

He paused, leaned forward and gripped my hand. 'I've got to say, Shona, it sounded fantastic! You sang it as though you meant every word, and now I know why – because *you* wrote those words. They're, quite simply, terrific. You must carry on and write more, and if my musical services can be of any help . . .'

He still hadn't let go of my hand. I was feeling hot and cold and shivery, and didn't know if it was because of my tonsillitis, or Rob. 'We ought to be getting back to the club, to see if anything's happened. We don't want the others agreeing to anything Mel tries to set up . . .' I pointed out.

'You're right. Okay, drink up.'

Hand in hand, we walked back to the Marquee, went round to the front, had a word with the girl on the desk, who recognized me, and went to find the rest of Zero. They were still in the bar. It wasn't so crowded there now because Male Order were onstage and most people had gone in to watch their performance. Mel and the two men were standing talking to Pip, Joss and Ireka, while the rest of our friends had found seats. *And Keith Randall had his arm round Kate!* I shot her a sympathetic look but she didn't even appear to notice.

All heads turned to look at us as we came in – and I was acutely conscious of my hand still enveloped in Rob's. I tried to pull away from him, but he was holding my fingers too firmly.

Mel gave me an ingratiating smile. 'Oh, Shona, I'd like to introduce you to two colleagues of mine, who you'll soon be working closely with. This is Eddie

Jackson of –'

'Hello, Mr Forty-five Per Cent – pleased to meet you,' I said sarcastically. 'You won't get away with it, you know. We're not as stupid as you think we are. We were intending to take any contracts we were given to a music business solicitor *of our choice,* to have them vetted before signing. And your generous deal would have gone right out of the window!'

'Shona!' exclaimed Pip. 'Whatever do you –'

'I overheard something I wasn't supposed to,' Rob butted in. 'I've advised Shona not to sign anything.'

'Listen, smart-ass, you can take that song of yours right out of the show. There's no way it's going to be the single now,' spat Mel, his eyes narrowed and flinty. He took a quick, angry swig of his drink and replaced the glass on the bar with a bang.

'It's my song, too – I think you're forgetting that,' I put in sweetly. 'And if I want to sing it . . .'

To my surprise, Dave Simmonds got to his feet and came striding over. He took Joss's arm, which amazed me even more. 'If we're driving all the way back to Liverpool tonight, I suggest we get going now,' he said. 'It'll be at least three before we get there. You can sort out your business problems on Monday.'

Monday . . . the day of that test! I thought with dread. How on earth was I going to get nearly three terms' work revised in one weekend – especially as I'd missed the last week of lectures and classes?

'It may have slipped your memories, but Zero has signed a management contract with me,' Mel said icily. 'For the next year, you'll do what I recommend, and I know a lot more about the business than you do.

Bloody artistic temperaments,' he groaned, turning to his henchmen. 'Don't you worry, we'll have this sorted out in no time. It'd be good to have that single in the shops before the summer.'

'What about our stuff?' I addressed Pip anxiously. 'Are we going back in the van, or what?'

'Well, I've sort of accepted a lift with Darryl and Ireka,' she answered, a bit sheepishly. 'I wanted to get away from gropey Tom.'

'Are you coming with me and Keith? Dave and Joss are,' Kate called over to me.

'Someone's got to stay with our gear,' I said desperately. 'What if it got ripped off?'

'Look, I'll come back in the van with you,' Rob suggested. 'I rather like the idea of letting someone else do the driving while we lounge in the back in the dark together. . . .'

His lips were close to my ear as he spoke and his words sent a thrilling chill darting down my spine. Did this mean he really wanted to be alone with *me*, though, or was I just a substitute for his girlfriend, who obviously hadn't been able to come tonight? I felt dreadfully confused, and to make matters worse my throat was now getting more sore by the second.

'I've got to go back to the hotel first and pick up my stuff. We all have. And please don't make me talk for a bit, until I've had some more pills and used the throat spray,' I hissed, with a pained grimace.

Mel said goodbye to us as if we were naughty kids. He hadn't even congratulated us on playing so well, I thought crossly. Fine manager he was! I'd always thought managers of any sort, whether sport or show-business, had it written into their job description that encouragement was just as important as criticism and business acumen.

Pip went off to drag Tom and Denis out of the main room, where they were lounging against the back wall with pints in their hands, watching Male Order and chatting up a couple of tarty-looking girls in very short leather skirts. They scowled and grumbled as they slouched towards us.

'I thought you'd all be staying down here for the weekend,' Tom groused.

'Sorry, we've just found out we've got an exam on Monday so we've got to get back to revise,' I explained, then wondered why I was bothering to be so polite. They'd never been exactly civil to us . . .

I didn't have much to pack at the hotel – I hadn't even *un*packed, except for my toothbrush and toothpaste. Then Pip made a suggestion. 'If we're not using our rooms, why don't we let some of the others have them? After all, Mel's paying . . .! I know Kate and Keith would love to have a weekend in London.'

'I'd like to stay,' piped up Ireka. 'That's if Darryl wants to, and it's all right by you, Shona . . .'

'If you want to go out with Darryl, go with my blessing,' I told her warmly. 'He's a fabulous guy, but there's never been anything between us, you can count on that. Anyway, I've got my eye on . . . er . . . somebody else.'

'It's all right, Shona, you don't need to get uptight about it.'

I whirled round and there was Joss, standing in the bathroom doorway, her sponge-bag dangling from her fingers and a towel draped over her shoulder.

'Maybe I owe you a few apologies. I was a bit of a bitch when Zero first got together. I'm sorry. I'd just had my heart broken by some unthinking, unfeeling swine, and I hated men and anything to do with them. But I don't feel so bad any more.' She gave an unexpected grin, which produced dimples in her cheeks and I realized that what I'd thought was just a newly-scrubbed face was, in fact, pink with a fiery blush!

'I think,' she went on, 'that I couldn't bear to see anyone else near me falling in love. It cut me like a knife. My emotions were red-raw. When I saw Kate around with Dave –'

She grinned again as she observed my expression. 'Yes, I was going out with Dave long before Kate was. We've known each other for years – we were childhood sweethearts, I suppose. Then he went and fell for your pretty friend and I suppose I took it out on you a bit, too. I really am sorry, Shona. Shake and be friends?'

She walked towards me, held out her hand and I shook it firmly. 'Of course,' I whispered. 'Hang on a mo.' I went and got my throat spray and gave my tonsils an almighty blast.

'Anyway, Dave and I are back together again now, though I'm sorry for Kate. It must have hurt her a lot.'

'Not as much as it might have done,' I filled in. 'She was more angry than anything. I don't think they were together long enough to fall deeply in love.'

'Someone seems to be cheering her up now,' Ireka said mischievously.

'If you think there could be anything between Kate

and Keith Randall – why, he's a great, hulking –'

'Teddy bear!' completed a voice from the doorway triumphantly.

'Kate!' My hand flew to my mouth and I blushed even more furiously than Joss had just done. 'I'm sorry. But look, please set everyone's minds at rest and stop the gossip right here. You don't actually . . . *like* Keith, do you?'

'Like him, yes. Fancy him . . . I don't think so, but he is sort of cuddly,' my mate said, grinning broadly. 'He's also the funniest bloke I've ever met. He's a laugh a minute, and it's great. I'll probably go around with him, but not *out*, if you know what I mean. I don't think he fancies me, in that way . . .'

All of a sudden, a certain conversation of ages ago returned to my mind. Keith had been pumping me for information about Kate . . . He *did* fancy her! I thought it tactful to say nothing about it. It was best to let them work it out for themselves.

'So,' I said, swallowing gingerly and prodding my painful neck glands, 'you and Ireka are having one room and Darryl and Keith the other.'

'Something like that,' Ireka said, and gave Kate a big wink.

'That's everyone sorted out then,' Joss said. 'I'll go back in Dave's car, and you and Rob'll go back in the van. I'll ring you tomorrow, Shona, to talk about this test.'

'Why don't you and Shona go round to my place in the morning, then you can copy out my notes. I'll ring Mum and tell her where they are,' Kate suggested helpfully.

I gave Kate a hug. 'You're magic,' I said affectionately.

Tom and Denis made a few ribald comments as I stuck our guitar cases on the spare seats in the front of the van in order to make room for two bodies on the blankets in the back. I was feeling very tired and I knew I wasn't at all well. But Rob got them to shut up and the minute he lay down next to me and wrapped his arms around me, I felt better. So much for romance, though. I dozed off almost immediately, and didn't wake up till we were on the outskirts of Liverpool, halfway through the night. Rob had wrapped the rather grubby blankets around me and was sitting hunched up, looking cold and sleepy.

I tried to say something to him, but my voice really had gone.

'I must get you home, you poor invalid,' he said.

In fact, I was very, very glad to crawl into bed, at four in the morning, having made myself a hot water bottle and taken my antibiotics religiously. I didn't know how I was going to swot the next day, feeling like this. I just hoped a few more hours' sleep would make me feel better. But the following morning I awoke feeling extremely feverish and light-headed. I struggled to the fridge and poured myself some orange juice, drank two full glasses, then draped a coat over my nightie and went, rubber-legged, down the stairs to the phone, where it took me about five attempts to dial Kate's number.

Somebody was just answering when I remembered, with a sinking heart, that Kate wasn't there, of course. She was still in London, disporting herself with Keith.

So I just croaked, 'Sorry,' and replaced the receiver and hobbled back to bed.

Chapter Seventeen

Looking back, I can recall a whole lot of faces, bobbing towards me, then away from me, like balloons in a breeze. Glasses were held to my lips for me to sip, and cool flannels mopped my hot face. I remember kicking the bedclothes off, and having them all plonked back on me again. There were awful draughts coming from somewhere, then I was red hot and gasping for air.

I don't know how many hours I was in that state, but it must have been dark by the time my eyes next focused properly, because my bedside light was on and Kate was sitting by me.

'Are you feeling better?' she asked anxiously.

I nodded weakly.

'I rang your doctor, but when he heard you were already taking antibiotics, he said there was no point in his coming round, but that you were to keep taking them and keep drinking lots of liquids. He said if you still had a temperature tomorrow, he'd look in, and that if your tonsils kept giving you trouble, you should go and see him, anyway.'

'I think — all the singing — just aggravated my throat,' I jerked out. My mouth was so dry, I felt like a camel that hadn't found an oasis for a fortnight.

'What time is it?' I enquired.

'It must be getting on for nine. I've been here ages — your downstairs neighbour let me in.'

'But what about my work? I'll never pass that test!' I wailed frantically, starting to clamber out of bed, though what good it would do me to start swotting now, I had no idea.

'Forget it,' Kate said firmly, pushing me back. 'You're in no fit state to do a shorthand test. I'll tell Gina you've genuinely got tonsillitis and I'll lie and say you've had it for a week and that you've been at home with your parents. She won't argue with that.'

'Thanks.' I smiled at her, thinking how wonderful she was to be able to solve my problems so easily. I was lucky to have her as my friend.

Then something struck me. It was Saturday, wasn't it? If so, what was Kate doing here when she should have been in London? Or had I lost a day in my delirium and it was Sunday already?

'Kate, please don't think I've gone mad, but what day is it?' I enquired.

A wry smile twisted the corners of her lips. 'I can guess why you're asking,' she replied. 'It *is* Saturday, and I got back at about eleven-thirty this morning. I . . . Well, you see, it was awkward, really. Ireka and your friend Darryl are obviously nuts about each other, but the same couldn't be said of me and Keith. I mean, I didn't want him to think I was throwing myself at him, and having to share a room would have put us both in a highly awkward position. So I'm afraid I left him a note while he was in the bathroom, and skedaddled.'

'But what time was this?' I gasped, horrified at the thought of my friend wandering around the capital in the middle of the night. *Anything* could have happened. The fact that she was here, intact, seemed like a miracle.

'About three, I suppose. We'd all just come back from a disco. I found an all-night café and sat there for a couple of hours, then found out from the waitress that Euston station was only just up the road. And, as luck would have it, there was an early morning train, not a through one, unfortunately – I had to change. But –'

She stopped and gave me a worried look. 'Perhaps I shouldn't have done that to Keith. I suppose he might have been hurt and upset. He is very sensitive, you know, beneath that jokey exterior. And if he *does* fancy me, then I suppose –'

'Sorry, Kate, but I'm afraid you have hurt him,' I informed her, and went on to tell her about the odd conversation I'd had with him.

'I'd better ring him, then, and apologize,' she said, reaching for one of the apples she'd brought me and sinking her teeth into it. 'Oh, by the way, you had a phone call yourself – from Rob. I answered and told him you were ill, and he made me promise to ring back later with a health bulletin. Any messages?'

I smiled. 'Just tell him he makes a really comfy pillow.'

Kate made sure I had everything I needed, then

borrowed my key so that she could let herself in the following day. But by the time I heard her footsteps coming up the stairs, I was already up, dressed and seated at the dressing-table with my shorthand notes propped up against a tin of talc, trying vainly to memorize what I hadn't taken much interest in in the first place.

'Huh!' Kate snorted when she saw me. 'Nurse Kate's come round, all prepared to minister to the sick, and I find my invalid has escaped! I really don't think you should be out of bed. You were in a terrible state yesterday.'

'I'm feeling a bit better and the pain in my throat isn't so bad,' I assured her. 'If only I could get this boring stuff into my brain.'

'Look,' she scolded, plucking the book from my grasp and closing it with a snap, 'we're going to stick to plan A, telling Gina you're ill. My mum'll vouch for you. I was so worried about you yesterday morning that I went and brought her over. You don't remember anything about it, do you?' she added, aware that I was looking at her puzzledly.

'Anyway, I've given Joss last week's lecture notes. She'll do her best to pass, and we'll do our best to make sure you don't get thrown out.'

I gave up. There was no arguing with her in this mood. She plonked herself on the edge of my bed. 'There was quite a bit of scandal you missed last week,' she started, but, like a fool, I butted in with, 'You mean Joss and Dave?' and then could have bitten my tongue out!

'Sorry,' I said awkwardly, but she just shrugged.

'Don't worry, I'm over Dave. And Joss and I have talked about it and we're the best of friends. She's really very nice, you know. She was just going through a bad patch. No, the scandal I meant was about Cathy Edgworth. She's left, and she's not going to take her exams. Rumour has it that it's all Pete Darby's fault, but I suppose we'll never know. Mind you, remember those love-bites?'

We both giggled. 'I suppose the boring truth is that she just got fed up with the course – or even got offered a job, lucky thing,' I said.

Kate shot me a meaningful glance. 'You'll never be out of work while you've got Zero,' she reminded me. 'I really think you've got a future there . . .'

'Some chance,' I joked, but all the same I found myself hoping, with a little thrill, that she might be right.

Kate went home for lunch, then came back with food for me.

'Mum says you need feeding up, so here's some cold chicken and salad, plus some ice cream. It's rather melted, I'm afraid.'

I wasn't feeling at all hungry, but the appetizing smell of the cold, spiced chicken wafted to my nostrils and I was suddenly ravenous. I was about to tuck in when someone rang the doorbell.

'Leave it, Kate – it's probably for someone in one of the other flats,' I said. But nobody else answered either, and it rang and rang insistently. In the end Kate got up and ran downstairs, saying it might be Joss or Pip.

But it wasn't. The person who walked in just when I was demolishing a chicken leg and was greasy from ear to ear, was Rob.

'Oh, no!' I spluttered, thinking what an awful, un-kempt sight I must look.

'That's a fine greeting! I can tell *you're* better,' he responded sarcastically, but with a twinkle in his eye. 'Any left over?'

'Sorry, you're too late. You can have a spoonful of vanilla mush, though,' I offered, passing him the plastic tub.

'Ugh!' He grimaced.

'Well, I must be off. I've got some work to do myself, after all,' Kate said.

I wanted to say, *don't go just because Rob's here,* but I couldn't, of course. She yelled, ''Bye,' and trotted off down the stairs, just as Bronski Beat came to an end on the cassette player.

'Could you turn it over?' I asked Rob.

'Do you mind if we don't just now? I'd rather like to talk,' Rob said mysteriously. Then he rummaged in a carrier bag he'd brought with him and took out a piece of paper which I instantly recognized. It was a copy of the contract Zero had signed with Mel Katz!

'Joss lent it to me so that I could study it, and it seems all is not lost,' he announced cheerfully. 'Here . . .'

He thrust it under my nose and I put the tub of ice cream down on the carpet and took it from him. He stood over me, squinted down at the paper, then pointed to a line.

'There! What does that say?' he asked triumphantly.

'*Subject to review after six months* . . . You mean that bit?'

'Yeah. That was obviously to give him an "out"

clause in case Zero weren't doing well, but it works in your favour, too. It means that, if you are not satisfied with him, you can vote to terminate the contract *after six months*! So, by August, you can be totally free of him.'

It sounded an awfully long time. 'But do we have to do everything he says until then?' I had visions of him making us play at holiday camps in July, dressed in bikinis.

'You won't be *able* to do much from now till the end of term, anyway. You've got your diploma exams, haven't you?' he reminded me. 'When he took you on, he understood that you were students, so he's got to expect music to take a back seat for the next few weeks.'

I instantly felt more cheerful. 'So we won't need to rehearse nearly every night . . . We'll have more time to write new songs, too. But—' I looked at him, worry and appeal in my eyes ' — if we get rid of Mel, we'll have to start all over again, find a new manager, start the same old rounds of rotten clubs, foul-mouthed roadies, or, even worse, borrowing Pip's cousin's lethal van again. I don't know if I could stand all that.'

I sighed and pulled my dressing gown more tightly around me in case my grotty old nightie was showing — or, even worse, any glimpses of my chest! 'We might as well give up. As you said, we've all got exams to pass. And what then? We'll all be leaving, going our separate ways, getting jobs . . . We mightn't all stay in Liverpool. I can just imagine Pip going off to join the Greenham Common women or something. It was a stupid idea really, starting Zero; it's brought us zero money, zero luck. Perhaps we should have called ourselves Zillion instead — then we might all have been rich by now!'

My gloom was increasing. 'I suppose we'll call it a day, give up the idea of fame and fortune. Wanna buy a guitar, going cheap?'

I was gazing, doom-filled, at the carpet as I said all this. Suddenly I felt a warm hand gently take my chin and tilt it upwards.

'Silly girl.'

I was about to protest, when Rob's mouth came down on mine in a kiss that was at first firm, then gentle and exploring, brushing my lips softly and sensitively until I grew dizzy, forgetting to breathe.

I let out a long sigh as he released me, too overcome to look at him. Why had he done this? I thought bitterly, as the magic started to recede. Why tease me so cruelly, and awaken all those emotions I'd tried so hard and so long to forget?

'It's wonderful to feel free to kiss you, Shona. I've been wanting to for so long,' he murmured.

'How could you, when you had a girlfriend?' I ground out from between clenched teeth. Oh, this was torture! I couldn't bear it if he was about to lie to me and start trying to two-time her and me.

'Girlfriend?' he said, his voice puzzled. 'I haven't got a girlfriend. I don't know what you're talking about. The reason I haven't exactly pursued you before is that you never gave me any encouragement, apart from all the business with the band and Joss's silly rules . . .'

I seized his wrist. 'Don't lie to me, Rob! What about that night when I was round at your digs and that girl came?'

'Oh, you mean Barbara.' He looked amused. 'Look at me, Shona.'

'No, I won't,' I protested wildly, shaking my head. If I gazed into those eyes just once, it would be all over and I'd be back to being miserable and lonely and suffering all the pangs of unrequited love — and I could do without that, with my final exams coming up!

'*Look* at me.' His voice was compelling and my anguished grip on his wrist slowly released as, reluctantly, I raised my eyes to his.

'That girl was Barbara Matthews. She's doing the same course as me and right at the beginning we made a deal that, to save money, we'd buy all the textbooks we needed between us, and share them. She came round to give me my turn at *The Practical Application of Stress Ratios.*'

He laughed and as he moved his head, his hair was suddenly outlined in glinting gold, like a halo.

'It's a nice day!' I exclaimed in surprise, getting up and pulling back the curtains to reveal wonderful sunshine that not only flooded the room, but seemed to flood me, too.

'Okay, I believe you. Will you forgive me for being so stupid?' I begged.

Rob kissed me again. 'Of course I will, dumbo! Now listen carefully, because I've got a proposition to put to you. What do you think Zero would say if I said I wanted to manage you? My father's an accountant, you know, so I don't think I'd get many sums wrong. *And* I could keep you supplied with melodies for your songs . . .'

I closed my gaping jaw, then stuttered: 'I think – I think it would be wonderful! But wouldn't you rather re-join us and be on stage again?'

Rob shook his head. 'Joss and Pip were right, you *are* better as an all-girl outfit. It'll get you far more attention and publicity – and you're *good,* believe me! You don't need me. Your guitar playing's coming on in leaps and bounds.'

I gazed at him, all sorts of fantastic scenarios playing through my head.

'I think that, once exams are over, you should ignore anything Mel says and rehearse and write like mad, and once that contract runs out, you'll be ready for anything. I would love to be part of getting Zero to the top.' Rob put his arm round me and gave me a hug. 'Can I take my favourite guitarist out to the movies as soon as she's well enough?' he enquired.

'You bet!' I breathed.

'There's just one thing, though.' Rob's voice was deadly serious and a pang of anxiety shot through me. Then I looked into his eyes and saw the teasing twinkle there.

'I'm not going to be just a *chapter,*' he murmured. 'Oh no. I'm going to stick around for the whole book!'